Mary-Kate and Ashley
Sweet 16

CROSS OUR HEARTS

By Eliza Willard

📖 HarperEntertainment

An Imprint of HarperCollinsPublishers

A PARACHUTE PRESS BOOK

A PARACHUTE PRESS BOOK

Parachute Publishing, L.L.C.
156 Fifth Avenue, Suite 302
New York, NY 10010

Published by
HarperEntertainment
An Imprint of HarperCollins*Publishers*
10 East 53rd Street, New York, NY 10022-5299

ISBN 0-06-052814-1

First printing: April 2003

Printed in the United States of America

Visit HarperEntertainment on the World Wide Web at
www.harpercollins.com

10 9 8 7 6 5 4 3 2 1

chapter one

"Oof!" I grunted as my belly slapped the water. My surfboard lunged toward the shore.

"Another wipeout!" Brittany cried, laughing. "What happened, Ashley? Even Lucas could've handled that wave."

"Thanks," I snapped. Lucas was Brittany's baby brother. He was barely a week old.

I managed to catch my surfboard and stumble onto the beach. I plopped down on the sand next to Brittany Bowen, one of my best friends—and a great surfer. Little droplets of water sparkled on her short curly hair and long brown arms.

It was a beautiful Saturday afternoon, perfect for surfing. Brittany was breaking in her new board and teaching me a few tricks. It was the first chance she'd had to go surfing since Lucas was born.

"You look pretty sloppy out there," Brittany said.

I knew she was right. I was no surf pro, but I hadn't been *this* bad in a long time.

"I can't concentrate," I explained. "My mind's just not on the waves."

"It's Aaron, isn't it," Brittany guessed.

I nodded. My first date with Aaron Moore was that night and I couldn't stop thinking about it.

"I want everything to be perfect tonight," I confided. "But I haven't had any time to get ready. I don't even know what I'm going to wear! I spent the whole morning planning this dinner for my dad—"

"What's going on with your dad?" Brittany asked. "Is it his birthday or something?"

I shook my head. "He got a major promotion at the music company where he works. Senior vice president of marketing and synergy. Whatever that means . . ." I shrugged. "It's a big deal, so I want to throw him a celebration dinner. He deserves it."

"Ashley," Brittany said, "we could have gone shopping for your date this afternoon instead of splashing around in the ocean. Why didn't you say something?"

"You've been dying to try out your new board," I explained. "And you've been so busy helping your mom with Lucas . . . I thought you could use a day at the beach."

Brittany laughed. "That is so typical. You're

always putting other people ahead of yourself—me, your dad. . . ." She shook her head. "When I asked Mary-Kate she told me she was busy and tried to corral me into helping her find good places to shoot her contest picture. She said, 'As long as you're at the beach anyway . . .'"

"I know—she said the same thing to me." I grinned. "I think it's great that she's entering that *Infocus Magazine* contest. I bet she'll win, too. She's really *on a roll!*"

Brittany groaned. "Very funny—*not.*"

I thought about all the great things Mary-Kate had done in the last few months. She starred in the school play, won a prize with her photos at the art show, joined the school Website staff. . . . And she was always telling me that I should get more involved in that kind of stuff, too.

And that's just what I'm going to do, I decided. "You know what," I said to Brittany. "From now on I'm going to be more like Mary-Kate—you know, really think big and do more with my talents."

Brittany jumped up. "You know what my idea of thinking big is? A *big* chocolate shake. Come on. Race you to the snack bar!"

❀

"Come on, cough it up, you greedy little file-gobbler!" I slapped the side of my laptop computer. The screen just blinked at me.

3

"You won't have Mary-Kate Olsen to kick around much longer," I threatened. "Someday I'll buy a new laptop, and where will you be then? Huh? Huh?"

I was right in the middle of writing an article about after-school activities, when my laptop swallowed my notes. No matter what I did, I couldn't access them. It was Saturday afternoon, and the article was due to be posted on the school Website by Monday morning.

I desperately stabbed at the keyboard. No good. The notes had disappeared. "Ugh! I hate you!" I shouted.

I shook my head, trying to clear it. What was I doing? Yelling at my computer? These Website deadlines were really getting to me.

"Are you busy, Mary-Kate?" I turned away from my laptop to see Mom leaning in the doorway of my room, purse slung over her shoulder.

Busy? Was she kidding? Besides trying to finish the Website story, I had a history test to study for, an English paper to write, *and* I had to shoot, develop, and print a prize-winning picture for the amateur photographer contest in *Infocus Magazine* by next Friday's deadline. I didn't know how I was going to get everything done in time.

"Well—" I began.

"I hate to bother you, but I really need someone

to give me a hand with some errands," Mom said.

Mom's car was in the shop—again. Did the machines of the world have some kind of vendetta against me?

"Would you mind driving me into town?" she asked. "I was going to ask Ashley, but I think she and Brittany went surfing. It shouldn't take too long."

I glanced at my enemy, the laptop. There wasn't much I could do about the lost notes now. Maybe the laptop would fix itself while I was out helping Mom run errands.

Sure, I thought. *Little elves will come out of my closet and fix everything. My bed will be made, my clothes hung up, my homework done. . . .*

"Okay," I agreed. I knew Mom wouldn't ask if it wasn't important. And after all, I wouldn't even *have* a car if it weren't for her and Dad. They gave Ashley and me a pink Mustang convertible for our sixteenth birthday—and we love it. The least I could do was give Mom a ride to town.

I scooped up my bag and my car keys and we headed out to the 'Stang. "Where to?" I asked Mom.

She pulled out a list. "I guess we should start at the mall."

"The mall it is," I said. But as soon as we pulled off our street, we hit traffic.

"What's going on?" I asked. Saturday traffic in

Malibu could be bad, but it usually wasn't *this* bad.

"Looks like there's a broken stoplight at the corner," Mom said.

"Great," I grumbled. "This could take all day."

And it did. We went from the mall to the stationery store to the supermarket, and every time we pulled out of a parking lot, we got stuck in traffic. My nerves were wearing thin.

"I wish we could fly through the air over all these cars," I complained. "When are they going to invent jetpacks? I mean, come on! It's the twenty-first century! I thought we'd have them by now!"

Mom laughed, but I wasn't trying to be funny. If one more car cut me off, I was going to scream.

"Relax, honey," Mom said in her soothing voice.

I breathed deeply, trying to calm down.

"What do you think of these invitations?" Mom asked. She pulled some note cards out of a bag as we sat at a stoplight. The cards had a fancy red and gold paisley design and the word *Celebrate!* written on them in pretty lettering.

"They're nice," I said. "What are they for?"

"Didn't I tell you? Ashley had a great idea this morning. We're throwing your dad a big dinner to celebrate his promotion! Ashley's taking care of all the details. She's going to plan the menu, cook the dinner, and everything."

"That *is* a great idea," I said, feeling a pang of

guilt. It was just like Ashley to think of something nice to do for Dad. Why didn't I ever have great ideas like that?

"Don't say anything to your father," Mom warned. "It's going to be a surprise. He's leaving on a business trip next week, and his promotion doesn't become official until he gets back. So we'll have plenty of time to plan the party and surprise him!"

Honk-honk! The guy in the SUV behind me blasted his horn. The light had turned green.

"Keep your pants on," I muttered. I pressed the gas pedal and drove through the intersection, only to stop dead in bumper-to-bumper traffic once again.

"Doesn't Ashley have a big date tonight?" Mom asked. It amazed me how the traffic didn't seem to bother her at all. She acted as if she were relaxing at home in the living room.

"She's going out with Aaron Moore," I told her. "That guy she found through her matchmaking service at Click. She applied her Theory of Compatibility to him and they got a great score."

"I don't know about that theory of hers," Mom said. "But Aaron sounds like a nice boy."

"He is," I said. "Ashley's really excited about it— but I think she's a little nervous, too."

She only went surfing for Brittany's sake, I realized.

That's just like Ashley, too. . . . I should try to be more like her.

The SUV behind me honked again. "If that guy honks at me one more time, I'm going to puncture his tires," I grumbled.

Mom patted me. I sighed. If I really wanted to be like Ashley, I had a long way to go.

❀

"How about this?" I asked Mary-Kate, twirling in front of her in a lacy black dress. "Too fancy?"

"Where is Aaron taking you? Capretto's?" she asked.

I nodded. Capretto's was a lively family-run Italian restaurant nestled in the hills.

"Then it's way too dressy," Mary-Kate declared. "What about your baby-blue wrap dress?"

"Perfect," I agreed, riffling through my closet.

"So how was surfing with Brittany today?" Mary-Kate asked.

"Terrible!" I told her. "I wiped out big time. But she's getting good. You know something Mary-Kate? I was thinking . . ." I paused, remembering how I vowed to be more like her, do more with my talents.

"I was thinking about something today, too," Mary-Kate said. "Mom told me about your plans for Dad's dinner, and it's such a great idea. You know something? I wish I could be more like you."

I laughed. Mary-Kate and I were on the same wavelength—even when we were trying to be different. "I was just going to say the same thing!"

The doorbell rang. "Is it seven o'clock already?" I cried, glancing at the clock. "He's here!"

chapter two

"I have a confession to make, Ashley," Aaron said. He leaned back in his chair and wiped a bit of tomato sauce off his lip. We had a corner table at Capretto's and were polishing off big bowls of spaghetti. "You probably don't remember this, but I had a huge crush on you in kindergarten."

"Kindergarten?" I racked my brain, trying to remember all the boys I knew in kindergarten. I didn't remember a boy named Aaron. "Were you in my class?"

"No, I was in Mrs. Carpenter's class." He brushed his bangs away from his dark blue eyes. *He's so cute,* I thought as I watched him talk. Tall, athletic, his dark hair kind of shaggy and long. . . . No wonder so many girls liked him.

"Your class put on that Thanksgiving pageant," Aaron explained. "And our class came to watch—"

"Oh, no," I gasped. "Not that!" I knew exactly

what he was talking about. I was the star of our kindergarten Thanksgiving pageant—I played the turkey.

"You looked so cute in that turkey costume," Aaron said. I wasn't sure if he was serious or teasing me. "With all those feathers sticking up on your head . . ."

"Stop it!" I cried. "Enough!" I couldn't believe he remembered this.

"I bet you don't remember your lines," Aaron teased.

Who could ever forget? "'Quack quack quack!' I forgot my lines, so I improvised."

Aaron laughed. "And that girl from my class stood up and yelled, 'That's not what the turkey says! The turkey says gobble-gobble! The duck says quack!'"

I covered my face with my hands. "I felt so stupid. I knew that turkeys don't say quack. But I was so nervous. I ruined the play!"

"Are you kidding?" Aaron said. "That was the highlight of the show. You brought the house down."

"Yeah, great," I said through my laughter. "Except the play wasn't supposed to be funny. It was the end of my kindergarten acting career. My teacher didn't let me have a speaking part in a play for the rest of the year."

The waiter cleared away our empty pasta bowls and asked, "Can I get you some dessert?"

"I feel like ice cream," Aaron said. "Let's go to King Kone."

"Sounds good," I agreed.

King Kone was a funky old ice cream stand that had been around since the 1950s. You couldn't miss the giant blue gorilla out front. Aaron got a chocolate-chocolate dip and I got a choco-vanilla swirl. We perched on top of a picnic table under the buzzing neon lights and watched the little kids line up for cones with their parents.

"My mom used to bring me here after I went to the dentist," Aaron told me. "I always had a cavity and the dentist told her I should cut down on sweets. But she felt so sorry for me feeling so miserable that she couldn't drive past King Kone without stopping." He opened his mouth to show off two rows of shiny silver molars. "And that's why my mouth is the silver mine you see today."

"I never had a cavity," I reported. "Mary-Kate has some. It drives her crazy."

A new silver Mercedes sports car pulled into the King Kone parking lot.

"Oh, no." Aaron groaned.

"What?" I asked.

A tall, pretty girl with long red hair climbed out of the car. A good-looking, sandy-haired guy stepped out of the passenger side. The girl spotted Aaron and waved. She and her friend came right over to us.

"Hi, Aaron," the girl said. She had beautiful green eyes.

"Hi, Meredith," Aaron said. "What's kicking?"

"This is David," Meredith said, nodding toward the guy she was with. "We're just grabbing a couple of cones."

"Cool," Aaron said. "This is Ashley." He put his arm over my shoulder. I was surprised. But it felt nice. And Meredith definitely noticed it.

"So what's new?" Meredith asked. "I haven't seen you in a while."

"Nothing much," Aaron said. "School. Soccer. You know."

"I'm going to Paris soon," Meredith said. "My dad wants me to spend a year learning French before I go to college. Maybe we could get together. I'd like to see you before I leave."

"Yeah, maybe," Aaron said. He stood up and led me toward his car. "Well, we've got to go. See you."

We climbed into Aaron's blue vintage Charger and drove off.

"Who was that?" I asked. "An old girlfriend?"

"Not really," Aaron said. "We went out a few times. But I wouldn't really call her a girlfriend." He pulled off at a scenic overlook with a view of the ocean. He turned off the car and we sat quietly for a minute.

"I've never really had a girlfriend," he said. "I mean, I've been out on a lot of dates with a lot of girls. But I've never really had one girl as my girlfriend before."

"Why not?" I asked.

He shrugged. "I just never found the right girl." He turned toward me and gazed into my eyes.

The light from the streetlamp glowed on his face. He leaned close and kissed me. I closed my eyes and kissed him back. He smelled like chocolate ice cream.

"Quack," I said when we broke apart. "Quack quack."

"He remembers you from kindergarten?" Mary-Kate said. "That's amazing!"

"I know." I sighed. As soon as I got home from my date with Aaron, I went straight to Mary-Kate's room. I sat beside her on the bed. "Mary-Kate, it was the most perfect date of my life. He's so cool! And so sweet!"

"But what about that red-haired girl?" Mary-Kate asked. "Doesn't that make you a little nervous?"

"A little," I admitted. "But he handled it really well. He made it obvious that I was with him on a date, and it kind of seemed as if he didn't really like her. Anyway, she was with another guy."

"If he put his arm around you in front of her, that's a sure sign," Mary-Kate said. "He's definitely not interested in her. And he definitely likes *you*."

I jumped up and twirled around on the floor. "I'm so happy!" I exclaimed. "I think Aaron is the perfect guy for me. And it's all because of my Theory of Compatibility! The theory must be genius!"

I came up with the Theory of Compatibility one day in math class. It was my special matchmaking system and it all had to do with ratios.

There were two categories—"Who I Am & What I Like" and "Who I Want to Be & Stuff that Matters to Me"—otherwise known as Interests & Personality and Goals & Values. It wasn't so important to have a lot in common with a guy. It was the ratio of common interests to common values that mattered. So if you had no common interests or values at all, you might get along great! I knew couples like that.

Or if you had five common values and five common interests, that would work, too. But an unbalanced ratio was a bad sign. Of course, if you and a guy had the same favorite book and the same favorite song, you were automatically a good match. I called that "The Clincher."

I made up a questionnaire people could fill out so I could chart their scores. Aaron filled one out, and his score matched mine perfectly! And now that we'd had our wonderful first date, I knew my theory was right.

"I should do something with this," I said, settling down next to Mary-Kate. "I mean, if you had a successful theory like this, you wouldn't leave it at that. You'd take it a step further. Wouldn't you?"

"I guess . . ." Mary-Kate said. "But how? You've already matched up just about everybody who goes to Click." Click was our favorite café and my matchmaking base of operations.

"What if we went beyond Click?" I said, thinking out loud. "To the Web! The school Website! Then everybody at school could do it!"

"That's not a bad idea," Mary-Kate said. "You could post your questionnaire on the site, and kids could fill it out on the computer—"

"—which could compute their scores automatically!" I was getting excited. "You could find your ratio with anybody else on the site instantly!"

"It's brilliant," Mary-Kate agreed. "I think Ms. Barbour is going to love this."

Ms. Barbour was the teacher who ran the school Website. She was glamorous and a little intimidating. But she was a big fan of Mary-Kate's work.

"The thing is, we'll need to get a lot of people to sign on right away," I said. "It won't be any fun unless you have plenty of matches to choose from."

"We'll advertise it on the Website," Mary-Kate suggested. "And how about this—what if I write an article about the theory? I'll find all the happy couples you matched up at Click and do a piece about how well your theory worked for them. Everyone in school will be dying to try it out!"

"I love it!" I cried. "This is so exciting!"

"Wow," Mary-Kate said. "I don't think I've ever seen you like this before."

"Get used to it, Mary-Kate," I said. "This is the new me."

chapter three

"What's that yellow thing?" Mary-Kate asked, staring through the mobs of kids in the hallway. We were walking into school on Monday morning, and something was stuck to the front of my locker.

As we got closer, I saw what it was—a yellow magnet shaped like a duck, with a note underneath.

"Who's it from?" Mary-Kate asked, but I already knew.

I opened the note. "Meet me for lunch today? The courtyard, fifth period—Quack."

"Wow," I sighed. A rush of happiness shot to my head so fast, it made me dizzy. "It's from Aaron. He wants to have lunch with me."

"Why did he sign it 'Quack'?" Mary-Kate asked, reading over my shoulder.

"Inside joke," I explained. "Kindergarten? The Thanksgiving play?"

Mary-Kate laughed. "You've been on only one

date and you've already got inside jokes! Aaron must be crazy about you!"

"I told you we're made for each other," I said. "Brought together by the scientific precision of my brilliant Theory of Compatibility."

Mary-Kate laughed. "All right, Dr. Ashley, Ph.D. The bell's going to ring any minute and I've got to get started on my English paper. See you later. Don't forget to meet me at the Website office after school."

She hurried off. I folded the note and put it in my bag. *This is going to be a great day,* I thought. *I can just tell.*

"Let's sit outside," Aaron suggested. "I know a great place." He led me to a shady spot under a tree in the courtyard. We leaned against the tree and unpacked our lunches.

"Mmm—my mom makes the best chicken salad," he said through a mouthful of sandwich. "She puts these Indian spices in. . . . Here, have a bite."

He held out the sandwich. I leaned forward and took a bite.

It was delicious, with almonds and raisins and curry powder. "That's good," I agreed.

"Want some more?" he offered.

I shook my head. "My pasta salad isn't bad

either, you know." I speared some pasta and gave him a bite. "Like it?"

He nodded, swallowed, and opened his mouth again. "More please."

I smiled and gave him another bite. I couldn't believe how comfortable I felt with Aaron after only one date. And he seemed at ease with me, too.

"Hey, guys." Lauren Glazer, one of my best friends, sat down beside us and opened her brown paper lunch bag. "Pretty day, huh?"

Lauren was tall and freckle-faced with long, wavy brown hair and a sunny personality. She looked happy. She usually did.

"Do you want to come over to Brittany's house after school today?" she asked me. "She's baby-sitting Lucas and I told her I'd keep her company."

"I can't," I replied. "I have a meeting with Ms. Barbour in the Website office this afternoon. I have a great idea for a new column—a matchmaking feature!"

Aaron started laughing. "That is such a cool idea," he said. "You'll do your Click thing online, right?"

"Exactly," I said. "You fill out the questionnaire, click on an icon, and presto! My theory calculates your perfect match."

"What a great idea," Lauren said. "Can you really program computers to do that?"

"Are you kidding?" I said. "Computers can do anything! I think. Actually, I've got to find somebody to help me program this thing." I glanced at Aaron.

"Don't look at me," he said. "I can't do anything on the computer unless my little sister shows me how."

"Hey—why don't you ask Malcolm?" Lauren suggested. "He troubleshoots all the computers at Click."

I paused. Malcolm Freeman worked behind the coffee bar at Click. He was very smart. I was sure he'd know how to create the program I wanted. I just wasn't sure he'd be willing to help me. He wasn't a big fan of the theory.

"Hey, Moore." Jim Hawley, a friend of Aaron's, stood over us, tapping a Frisbee against his knee. "Play a little catch?"

"Definitely." Aaron leaned over and kissed me on the cheek. Then he jumped to his feet and joined his friends on the field.

My cheek felt hot on the spot where he'd kissed it. "Wow," Lauren said. "Ashley, I think you've got yourself a boyfriend."

The warmth spread over my whole face. "I know," I said. "Isn't it great?"

Lauren watched him toss the Frisbee to his friends. "It's amazing," she agreed. "Aaron was the guy no girl could catch—and you converted him!"

"Hey, dudettes." Malcolm joined me and Lauren under the tree. "Excuse me while I puke up my lunch. They call it beef stew. I call it barf stew. Bleh." He leaned over and made fake barfing noises. His lank brown hair fell over his pale face.

Lauren rolled her eyes. "Please, I'm trying to eat here."

"I always pack my own lunch on beef stew days," I said. "You have to check the lunch schedule."

"Remind me to nominate you for a Nobel Prize," Malcolm said. "The Nobel Prize for Excellence in Lunch Planning. Or should it be matchmaking?"

He walked right into it. "Speaking of matchmaking . . ." I began. A look of disgust crossed Malcolm's face, but I didn't let that stop me. "I need a favor, Malcolm. Could you help me set up a matchmaking program on the school Website?"

"I could if I really wanted to," Malcolm said. "Unfortunately for you, I don't want to."

"Come on, Malcolm," I begged. "My fabulous Theory of Compatibility can bring happiness to hundreds of kids!"

Malcolm wasn't a big laugher, but he kind of barked out a "ha!"

"Misery, you mean," he said.

"It worked great for Ashley," Lauren said.

"And Mary-Kate is interviewing other couples who got together because of the theory, too," I said.

"Just because you're not into it doesn't mean you shouldn't help me."

"All right, I'll help you," Malcolm agreed. "But will you let me stick some funny bugs in the program? You know, like you click on 'FIND MY MATCH' and a skull and crossbones appears? Maybe a flashing red light that says 'Danger! Danger!'"

"No," I said. "No, you can't. But if you help me, I'll bring you something yummy for lunch every day for a week. How's that?"

"Better than nothing," Malcolm said. "It's a deal."

"A matchmaking column on the school Website," Ms. Barbour said. "'Ashley's Love Link.' Hmmm . . ."

I glanced at Mary-Kate while my stomach fluttered nervously. She flashed me a reassuring smile. Ms. Barbour was crisp and matter-of-fact— the kind of person you don't want to disappoint. Mary-Kate was used to that. But I still felt jittery around her.

"I'm looking up some of Ashley's matchmaking clients," Mary-Kate told Ms. Barbour. "I thought I could follow up on them, see how they're doing. We could post an article about the success stories as a way of advertising the new matchmaking feature."

Ms. Barbour studied the sample questionnaires

and graphs I'd brought to show her. "I like it," she finally said. "It's bound to bring a lot of attention to the site. Ashley, this is an excellent idea."

I grinned with relief. She liked it!

"I'd like to get started on this right away," Ms. Barbour added. "Are you ready for some hard work?"

"I'm ready," I replied. I couldn't stop smiling.

❀

"Hello, Kristen? This is Mary-Kate." As soon as I got home from school that day, I started researching my piece on Ashley's theory. My information said that Ashley had applied her theory to match Kristen Carson with a guy named Bob McSweeney. So I gave Kristen a call.

"Hi, Mary-Kate," Kristen said. "What's up?"

"I'm doing some research for Ashley," I explained. "I see that you filled out a questionnaire at Click a little while ago. So how are things going with Bob McSweeney?"

"You mean Bob McCreepy?" Kristen snapped. "Lousy!"

Click.

"Hello?" I said. It sounded as if she'd hung up on me! But that couldn't be. "Hello?"

No answer. She actually hung up!

Hmmm, I thought. *That didn't go very well. I wonder what's wrong with her? Let me try this next person. . . .*

The next name on the list was Bob McSweeney. I was kind of curious to hear his side of the story. I dialed his number.

"You talked to Kristen?" Bob asked.

"Um, well, I didn't exactly *talk* to her—" I said.

"She's a snob," Bob told me. "An anti-reptilist."

"A what?"

"She's prejudiced against reptiles. She told me she has nightmares about them. Phobias. So I figured I'd cure her. I brought my pet boa constrictor on our date, and she screamed! Right in front of Bob Jr.! She really hurt his feelings, and scared him a little, too. . . ."

I had to ask. "You named your boa constrictor Bob Jr.?"

"He's very friendly," Bob said.

I shuddered. "Well, I think I can see where you and Kristen went wrong. Thanks for your help, Bob."

"Anytime. Hey, you're not into reptiles, are you? I've got pet frogs, too—"

"Maybe next century. Good-bye, Bob."

Wow, I thought as I slammed down the phone. *Bob really* was *McCreepy. And McCrawly.*

I scanned my list and called Matt Anoki.

"Yeah, I went on one date with this girl, Alicia," Matt told me in a bored voice. "The thing is, I'm a goalie on the soccer team? And she thinks all jocks are morons."

This wasn't going too well, either. "Okay, so that date didn't work out," I said. "But did you think of trying again to see if you found a better match?"

"Not really," Matt said. "I didn't get the theory. I had nothing in common with Alicia—you could see it on our questionnaires. But somehow the theory said that was a good thing! Something about ratios. I just didn't get it. Basically, I just didn't want to go through it all again."

I tried a few more people. Stephanie Duarte told me her date got up to go to the bathroom in the middle of dinner and never came back. Bailey Lenhard, a senior, said her date was a freshman— he'd lied on his questionnaire. Oliver Peddy reported that his match was a dog—literally. Some guy had filled out the questionnaire for his dog as a joke.

This is terrible, I thought. *I can't find anyone who found a happy match through Ashley's theory.*

What's going on here? Is Ashley the worst matchmaker on the planet?

chapter four

"**O**kay, Ashley, here's how it works," Malcolm said. "Website users submit their photos to you. You scan the photos into the computer and click here to upload them. Or they can scan the pictures themselves if they know how."

It was Tuesday afternoon, and Malcolm was showing me the programming he'd done for "Ashley's Love Link." The kids who logged on would fill out the questionnaire and post their photos. Then they could scan through the other photos and questionnaires until they found someone they were interested in.

"Click on this star that says 'Match or Mismatch?'" Malcolm continued. "The computer automatically graphs their answers and compares them. If they have a good ratio, the screen flashes MATCH and the graph turns into a heart."

He clicked the mouse to show me how it worked.

Just as he said, the word MATCH in big pink letters flashed on the screen and the graph morphed into a pulsing red heart.

"That is so cool," I said. "What happens if it's a mismatch?"

"Watch," Malcolm said. He clicked again. A poison-green skull and crossbones filled the screen, with the words DANGER DANGER MUST AVOID flashing in black.

I laughed. "You found a way to use your skull-and-crossbones graphic after all," I said.

"Now check this out." He typed a command into the computer. A pop-up ad appeared. "This will pop up every time someone logs onto the school Website."

Next to a beating blue heart and a small picture of me were the words:

Do you get crushes on people, only to find out they're all wrong for you? Are you too stupid to choose your own dates? You need help! Check out our new feature, "Ashley's Love Link," debuting on Monday! Face facts. You know you're a loser—and the only person who'll ever like you is another loser just like you. Find that not-so-special someone on "Ashley's Love Link"! Monday! Monday! Monday! Be there! (You're already square.)

"Malcolm!" I protested. "I love the idea of the ad. But we've got to change the text."

"Gosh, I'm so hurt," Malcolm said sarcastically. "I had a feeling you were going to say that. Just type in this space to rewrite it."

"Thanks," I said. I thought for a moment. Then I wrote:

Check out "Ashley's Love Link," starting Monday! Find that special someone who's just right for you! Photos, questionnaires, graphs—we've got it all. Use Ashley's foolproof Theory of Compatibility to meet the guy or girl of your dreams. Monday! Monday! Monday! Be there!

Malcolm sighed. "I can't believe you roped me into setting up this site for you. Don't tell anyone I did it."

"Why not?" I asked. "It's so cool! Everyone will love it."

"I still say this whole matchmaking thing is for losers," Malcolm said. "Now for the important part—what did you bring me for lunch today?"

I pulled a neat brown paper bag out of my backpack. "How about leftover homemade pot roast with potato salad and a cupcake?"

"I won't say no." Malcolm reached for the bag and pulled out three small plastic containers. "Nice Tupperware, Ashley. Do I have to give it back?"

"Keep it," I said. "It's the least I can do. The Web page looks beautiful."

❀

"Hey, Rebecca, can I talk to you for a minute?" I cornered Rebecca Antrim in the locker room after gym. She was one of Ashley's Click matches.

Rebecca leaned down to tie her shoelaces. "Sure, Mary-Kate. What's up?"

"I'm doing a piece for the school Website on couples my sister, Ashley, matched at Click," I explained. "Sort of a follow-up story. So I was wondering, how are things going between you and Charlie Evert?"

Rebecca sat up. "It started out okay," she said. "I thought he was cute and everything. But then things went horribly, horribly wrong."

I sighed. I'd been hearing stories like this all day.

"What happened?" I asked.

"I saw him eat," Rebecca said. "Have you ever seen Charlie eat? He's a pig! He shovels food into his mouth as if he's afraid he'll never see another meal. It gets all over his face, all over his shirt. . . . It's disgusting. Egg salad is the worst."

I backed out of the locker room. "Okay, thanks, Rebecca," I said. I dreaded hearing the other side of *this* story. But I happened to run into Charlie outside the gym.

"I think there's something wrong with Rebecca," he reported. "She's a neat freak. Have you seen the way she eats?"

I shook my head and braced myself.

"She cuts everything up into tiny little pieces," Charlie told me. "Then she eats them, one teeny bite at a time. It takes her an hour to eat a slice of pizza. She should have her head examined!"

"Okay, thanks for the input, Charlie," I said. I hurried away and slumped on a bench in the courtyard. I was getting very nervous. I'd interviewed dozens of people, and I couldn't find a single happy couple out of all of Ashley's matches. Ms. Barbour wanted to see this article soon. What on earth was I going to do?

Then I spotted Sarah Hunter reading on the grass. She'd gone out with Warren Voigt since the ninth grade. To everyone's surprise, Sarah broke up with Warren. Ashley matched her with Toby Washburn, and so far, they seemed like the perfect couple.

Aha, I thought. *A happy couple at last*. Look out, Sarah, here I come.

I walked across the courtyard and sat down next to Sarah. She looked up from her book and smiled at me.

"How's it going, Sarah?" I asked.

She sighed. "I'm so depressed. You know that guy I was seeing, Toby?"

Oh, no, I thought. *Here we go again*.

"Yes," I said, crossing my fingers and hoping that this conversation wasn't about to go in the direction I thought it was. I held my breath . . .

"He dumped me!" Sarah complained, suppressing a sob. "He met some girl in his karate class that he likes. He said I wasn't spiritual enough. Can you believe that?"

My heart sank. Sarah was my best hope for a happy ending. And here she was, just another brokenhearted wreck.

"I really miss Warren," Sarah went on. "Now I know how he felt when I dumped him. But he won't take me back! He says it's too late. Mary-Kate, what can I do?"

"I bet Warren will take you back eventually," I told Sarah. "He's probably just trying to make you suffer. And maybe he wants to be sure you're really serious. He might be afraid you'll hurt him again."

Sarah brightened a little. "You're right. He doesn't have a new girlfriend yet. Maybe he's testing me."

"Give it a little time," I suggested. *This is weird,* I thought. *I actually sound as if I know what I'm talking about.*

Now for my problem. I still had an article to write—and not one happy couple to show for it. Except for Aaron and Ashley, of course.

They can't be the only ones, I thought. *Can they?*

"How's your matchmaking story going, Mary-Kate?" Ms. Barbour asked. It was the question I'd been dreading ever since I arrived at the Website office that afternoon.

"I can't wait to read it," she went on. "It will be the perfect companion piece to 'Ashley's Love Link.' We'll call it 'Happy Endings.'"

I swallowed and summoned up my nerve. "That's a terrific title," I said. "There's only one problem."

Ms. Barbour turned her sharp black eyes on me. "Problem? What is it?"

"Well, I've interviewed all the couples I can find," I began. "And I haven't found a single happy ending. Not one. Unless you count Ashley herself. She found a great guy using her theory."

Ms. Barbour frowned. "Not one happy couple? That's a pretty bad track record."

"Maybe we shouldn't do this story," I said. "Maybe we should just forget about it. No one will want to try the Love Link if they think Ashley's theory has, uh, a few glitches in it."

"I disagree," Ms. Barbour said. "Dating disasters are even more fun to read about than happy endings. I think the kids will be very interested in this story. I definitely want you to do it."

"But, Ms. Barbour," I protested. I was afraid the piece would embarrass Ashley—and that was the last thing I wanted to do. "It's not very good publicity for the Website."

"Nonsense. All publicity is good publicity. This is the kind of story that gets people talking. So if you don't want to do it, I'll assign it to someone else."

"No, no—I'll do it," I agreed. I didn't want to write the story. But at least I could make sure it caused as little damage as possible. Another writer wouldn't think of Ashley's feelings the way I would.

"Good," Ms. Barbour said. "Have it ready by Friday."

Friday. The last school day before Love Link's debut. What would Ashley say?

"Honey, can you read this?" Mom asked when I got home from school that afternoon. She was staring at some notes written in telltale purple glitter pen—definitely Ashley's writing. It was very neat, but she'd abbreviated so many words, it was hard to tell what she meant.

"What is it?" I asked.

"Ashley jotted down these notes when we were planning your dad's dinner the other day," Mom explained. "I have no idea what this says."

I struggled to read the abbreviations, but they were like code. "Maybe she was afraid Dad would see it and find out about the surprise," I said.

"Probably. The trouble is, she's kind of stopped working on the party. She's been so busy with that new Website thing she's doing, I told her not to worry about it." Mom sighed. "But now that we're expanding the day-care center, I don't know how I'm going to get everything done."

Mom ran a day-care center that was so popular, they were building an addition and adding extra classes. I knew she'd been swamped lately.

Hmm . . . Ashley's too busy to help Mom? I thought. *Maybe this is my chance to be helpful for once.*

"You know what, Mom?" I said. "I'll plan the party for you. I'll take over the whole thing—plan the dinner, cook it, send out the invitations—everything."

Mom looked startled. "You will?" she asked. "Are you sure you have enough time?"

I understood why Mom had her doubts. Sometimes I got in over my head by volunteering to do too much. Like the time I won the lead role in *Grease* and I ended up in charge of the sets and the costumes, too.

I *did* have a lot to do in the next few weeks. But I knew Mom needed help, and I really wanted to be there for her. And this was a party for Dad!

"You'll see, Mom," I promised. "I'll find the time."

Somehow.

chapter five

"Look at this guy," Malcolm said with his snorty laugh. "Who does he think he is, a model?"

Malcolm leaned over my shoulder as I pulled photos from my Click matchmaking notebooks to use as samples on the Website. He pointed at a picture of a boy whose long hair was blowing back even though the picture was taken indoors. And it looked as if he were sucking in his cheeks.

"Did he use a wind machine when he took that, or what?" Malcolm added.

"Stop making fun of my clients," I scolded, even though it *was* a funny picture.

"Listen to this." He pulled one of the questionnaires out of a pile. "'My most embarrassing moment was when I was nominated for Homecoming Queen.'" Malcolm read the entry in a fake girly voice. "'People I didn't even know stood up and said how beautiful and popular I am. It was so embarrassing!'"

I tried not to laugh. Of course the girl's answer was ridiculous. But I felt it was my duty to take my clients seriously.

"Hey—some of those questions aren't easy to answer," I said. "What would *you* write in that spot? Most embarrassing moment?"

"Look, nobody *has* to fill out a dating questionnaire," Malcolm said. "I'm smart enough not to do it in the first place. My most embarrassing moments will stay where they belong, locked deep inside my troubled soul."

He grinned so I knew he was at least half kidding.

"I think *you* should try the Love Link," I said. "Your questionnaire answers would be the smartest ones at school. I bet lots of girls would read them and think 'I want to date that guy.'"

"Sure," Malcolm said. "They'll say, 'I want to date that skinny, stringy-haired dude who reads a lot.' Girls love that."

"Some girls do," I insisted.

Malcolm patted my shoulder. "That's why I like you, Ashley," he said. "You have such a vivid imagination."

"Malcolm's pop-up ads are really working," I told Aaron later that evening. We were having dinner together at a seafood shack by the beach. "People are already talking about the Love Link. Although some kids don't quite get how it's set up. A few people have sent me personal ads."

Aaron snapped open a crab leg. "Like what?"

"Well, this one girl wrote, 'Freshman girl seeks boy, 14–16. Must be cute, good-looking, gorgeous, and extremely handsome.'"

"She's not shallow," Aaron joked.

"And then this boy wrote, 'Bayside senior, male, 18 years old, seeks girlfriend. Me: 5'10" brown hair, brown eyes, good speller, debate champion. You: female.'"

Aaron laughed. "Ashley, you quack me up."

"You're never going to let me forget that, are you?" I teased. "That horrible Thanksgiving pageant happened eleven years ago, and I'm still paying for it."

"I've got a long memory," Aaron said.

A waiter set a bowl of soup in front of me.

"What have you got there?" Aaron asked. "Clam chowder?" He passed the breadbasket to me. "Here, have some saltine quackers."

"Stop it!" I cried, laughing.

"I'm sorry," Aaron said. "It's just so much fun to tease you. I'll make it up to you. Here's a personal ad: Bayside junior, male, seeks kiss from cute blond classmate. Only girls named Ashley need apply."

I caught my breath and gazed into Aaron's blue

eyes. I'd never felt this way about anyone before. I leaned in and kissed him.

It was the most perfect kiss, ever.

❀

"Wow, you're home late," I said when Ashley knocked on my bedroom door. From the look on her face I could tell she'd had another great date with Aaron.

"I stayed late at school, getting the Love Link ready," Ashley explained. "Then I had to go to Click and pull some photos and questionnaires to use as samples. So I didn't get to meet Aaron for dinner until eight."

"And?"

She sighed happily and collapsed on my bed. "Fantastic. The more I get to know him, the more perfect he seems!"

"Wow," I said a little uncomfortably. I had some not so good news to break to her about the Love Link. I decided to start with some better news first.

"I know you've been really busy lately," I began. "So I offered to take over Dad's celebration dinner. Mom said she'd love the help."

Ashley sat up. "Mary-Kate, are you sure?" she asked. "I mean, that's not really your kind of thing, is it? And you're pretty busy, too, aren't you?"

"Why not?" I asked. "And anyway, what's so hard about planning a meal? How much time could it take? After all, people do it every day, you know."

She stood up and hugged me. "Thanks, Mary-Kate. I *have* been swamped lately. Just let me know if you need any help."

"I will," I said. Now that that was out of the way, it was time to bring up a touchier subject. "About that story I'm writing—the matchmaking follow-up?"

"How's it going?" Ashley asked. "Have you gotten lots of good love stories?"

"Not exactly," I confessed. "In fact, the only happy couple I could find was you and Aaron."

She blinked. "What? That's impossible."

"It's true," I assured her. "I couldn't find one couple you matched who was still together."

She sat on the bed in shock. "I can't believe it. Are you sure? Did you really look hard?"

I nodded. "Believe me, I tried. I told Ms. Barbour we should drop the piece, but she still wants to post it, horror stories and all. But, Ashley, I won't write it if you don't want me to."

"I just can't believe the theory didn't work," Ashley said. She sounded kind of stunned. "The idea behind it is right, I just know it is. It worked so perfectly for me. . . . I'd better go over it again and check it for kinks. Maybe I did the math wrong. Maybe I didn't figure the ratios right. . . ."

"Don't feel bad, Ashley," I said. "I'm sure there is some truth in the theory. You just have to dig it out."

She smiled at me. "Anyway, you should go ahead and write the article. Ms. Barbour will probably post the story whether you do it or not. So you might as well do it."

"Thanks, Ashley," I said. "Don't worry. I'll find a way to write it so it won't hurt your matchmaking rep. And as Ms. Barbour says, all publicity is good publicity, right?"

"I hope so," Ashley said. "I really want the Love Link to succeed. It's got to work. It's just got to."

chapter six

TALES OF HEARTBREAK AND WOE
by Mary-Kate Olsen

If you've been to Click Café recently, you know that my sister, Ashley Olsen, started a matchmaking system using her Theory of Compatibility. Many high school students came to Click, filled out questionnaires, had their pictures taken, and were matched with their fellow students.

How did it all turn out, you ask? Is Bayside High now full of happy couples cooing at each other like doves?

You have only to take a look around to see that the answer is no.

What went wrong? Here are a few examples. (Names have been changed to protect the guilty.)

Example #1: George went out with Lila. He liked her a lot. She told him she was afraid of snakes. This is a perfectly reasonable fear. Ask anyone. Snakes are scaly and slimy and sometimes bite.

So what did George do? He brought his boa constrictor on the next date. After that Lila never wanted to see him again. Can you blame her?

This is not the fault of matchmaking. This is the fault of George.

How could George have handled this differently? He could have listened to Lila and respected her wishes. There is no need for dating to involve boa constrictors.

Example #2: When 17-year-old Jane went to meet her date, Herman, she was shocked to discover that he was younger than she was. Three years younger. Yes, Herman was 14, a freshman. He was eager to pursue the relationship. Jane, however, was not interested. How did this happen? I'll tell you how. Herman lied! He lied about his age on his questionnaire. If you lie on your questionnaire, it will affect your score. Your matchmaker cannot interpret it correctly. Your match will not work!

There are many other ways to abuse the system.

Example #3: Victor, a sloppy eater, failed to follow proper mealtime etiquette on his date.

Example #4: Karen set up two dates for the same night. While on the first date, her second date called on her cell phone, telling her to hurry up and ditch Ron, her Click match. Ron's feelings were hurt. Anyone's would be. Karen's manners could use some work. But is this the fault of the Theory of Compatibility? I say no. It's the fault of you, the clients. Let's clean up our acts, people!

When you meet your match, be honest and considerate. Have good manners. Treat your date the way you'd like to be treated. Who knows? Maybe this time it will work out!

On Monday a new matchmaking feature, "Ashley's Love Link," debuts on this Website. Ashley has refined her famous theory and questionnaire to serve you better. As I know from long personal experience, Ashley has good matchmaking instincts and most of all really cares about people. So log on and let Ashley help you. Trust me, you need it. And when you fill out the questionnaire, be honest this time!

Ms. Barbour chuckled as she read my article. "Great job, Mary-Kate. Let's put it on-line."

44

I posted the article. *I hope Ashley will be happy with it,* I thought. *I did the best I could.*

❀

"Did you read Mary-Kate's article about your theory yet?" Malcolm asked. "It's hilarious."

"I guess so," I said. I was sitting at a computer terminal at Click on Friday night, desperately trying to work out the kinks in my theory. "Ashley's Love Link" was going to be up online Monday.

I didn't really find the story all that funny. But I appreciated Mary-Kate's take on it. It was nice of her to blame the theory's failure on the clients rather than on me. There was no way I could be mad about it.

And actually, I'd never thought of it that way before. Maybe Mary-Kate had a point. People couldn't expect me to make great matches if they weren't honest on their questionnaires. They had to take a little responsibility, too!

"The thing is, I really want the theory to work this time," I told Malcolm. "I want 'Ashley's Love Link' to be a success! Where do you think I went wrong?"

"You mean, aside from trying to match up a pack of lunatics in the first place?" Malcolm said. "For one thing, I don't think zero to zero is a ratio. Zero times zero doesn't equal one, it equals zero."

"You're right," I agreed. "From now on I won't

45

match up people who have nothing in common anymore. That should help avoid a lot of disasters."

"It's only logical," Malcolm agreed. "And what about this clincher thing? People who have the same favorite book and the same favorite song are automatically a good match? Where did that come from?"

I shrugged. "It just seemed right. I'm working on instinct here." I thought for a minute. "What if I throw in same favorite movie? That's got to mean something. And that would make the clincher pretty rare."

"Yeah, nobody ever likes the same movies," Malcolm joked. A customer waved at him from across the room. "Excuse me, Ashley. Somebody is beckoning me. I must attend to their needs." He slouched away.

I stayed late at Click, working to make the Love Link better. I appreciated what Mary-Kate had said in her article. But I didn't want people to make excuses for me. I wanted my theory to work. I wanted to match people up and make them happy—as happy as Aaron and I were.

"Hear that, Ashley?" Brittany asked as I walked down the hall at lunchtime on Monday.

"What?" I asked.

"That buzzing," Brittany said. "Listen."

I listened hard. Every few seconds I heard snatches of conversation. The words "Love Link," "Website," and "Ashley" popped up again and again.

"They're talking about your Web column!" Brittany exclaimed. "Nobody's talked about anything else all day!"

A boy I didn't know brushed past us. "Hey, it's Ashley Love Link!" he called.

I stretched up a little taller, excited and proud. It was really true! "Ashley's Love Link" was the talk of the school!

chapter seven

"**T**o the success of 'Ashley's Love Link!'" Mary-Kate cheered. She and Brittany, Lauren, and Aaron raised their coffee mugs in a toast. We'd all gathered at Click after school to celebrate the launch of my Web column.

"Thanks," I said, clinking mugs with them. "But it isn't a success yet. Today is only the launch."

"It will be," Lauren said. "Look around. Every computer in here is logged on to the Love Link."

I glanced around the café, and she was right. Kids were crowded around the monitors, filling out the questionnaires and trying to find matches.

"Hey—type this in," one boy said to another. "I was raised in a tree by apes, so I can love only an ape girl. You must be covered with fur."

The other boy typed the words and clicked on the star. "Let's see who gets matched with this! Calling all ape girls!"

48

I nudged Mary-Kate. "Did you hear that?" I said "They're treating the Love Link like a big joke!"

Three girls giggled at another computer nearby. "I can't believe you're taking this seriously, Katie," one girl said. "Didn't you hear what happened to Kristen?"

"Yeah—it doesn't work at all!" her friend said. "It's good only for laughs."

I stood up and cased the room, dashing from computer to computer. People were having a great time with the Love Link. The trouble was, none of them was taking it seriously! No one had any faith in my matchmaking skills!

I returned to my table, fuming. Aaron tried to distract me. "To Ashley!" he toasted again, raising his mug.

But I was in no mood for celebrating now. "The Website will never work if everybody uses it to play jokes on each other," I complained.

Malcolm stopped by the table to clear away empty glasses. "Hey, Ashley," he teased. "There's a guy over there trying to make a love connection with a *Star Trek* character."

Mary-Kate threw him a warning glance, but I caught it. She leaned close to me and whispered, "Don't worry. They'll stop fooling around soon and then they'll put your theory to the test for real."

"My theory works!" I declared. This was so

frustrating! "And I'll prove it somehow. Just wait!"

But I already had an inkling of how to prove my theory. Malcolm. The ultimate challenge. *If I can use my theory to match him with someone—and the match takes—no one will dare question it again. And the Love Link will be a success!*

"Anybody up for a walk on the beach?" Lauren asked.

"You all go without me," I said. "I've got something to do here. I'll catch up with you later."

Everyone stood up and got ready to go. Aaron put an arm around me. "Come on, Ashley. Don't you want to go to the beach and watch the sunset?"

He gave me a little squeeze. "Don't take this Love Link thing so hard," he whispered in my ear. "It will work out."

"I think I know a way to make it happen," I told him. "But I need a few minutes alone here first."

"All right," Aaron said. "Want to go to a movie later?"

I nodded. "Sure. See you later."

Everyone left. I sat alone at the table, watching Malcolm as he worked behind the counter washing glasses.

How should I approach him? I wondered. I knew he'd resist. *Well, I just won't take no for an answer,* I decided. *I'll be strong and determined. I'll make this work no matter what the obstacles.*

50

I marched up to the counter. "Malcolm, you have to help me."

"Now what is it?" he complained. "You need your hard drive cleaned? You want me to come to your house and mow the lawn?"

"Nothing like that," I assured him. "This will be fun."

"Sure it will," he said. "Okay. Lay it on me."

"Listen—*I* know my theory works. It matched me with Aaron, my perfect guy! But no one else believes in it. I need to prove once and for all that my theory is genius. And you've got to help me."

"How? I think your theory is nuts."

"Well, if that's true, you won't be afraid to try a little experiment."

"What experiment?" he asked warily.

"Fill out a questionnaire for me," I pleaded. "Let me try to make a match for you."

"Forget it."

"Please, Malcolm. What do you have to lose?"

"My dignity, for one thing. My sanity is another possibility."

"You're just scared," I insisted. "If I match you with someone you like, wouldn't that be a good thing?"

"I guess so," he said. "But I know that's not going to happen. So why should I bother?"

"Because if I *don't* make a match for you, it will

51

prove that you're right—and I'm wrong," I said.

His eyes lit up. I could tell that idea appealed to him. But he shook his head.

"No," he said. "I don't need to go through all that just to prove I'm right and you're wrong. I already know that!"

"Then you won't mind helping me out," I said. "Prove *to me* that you're right. Please, Malcolm. For me. Please just fill out the questionnaire."

Malcolm sighed. "If I do it, will you stop bugging me about it?"

"Yes."

"All right," he agreed. "I'll fill out the stupid questionnaire for you. But that doesn't mean I'll go on any dates. I'm just filling out the form. Okay?"

"You promise to fill it out for real? Not as a joke?"

"Yes, I promise."

"Thank you, Malcolm! You won't be sorry."

"Oh, yes, I will," he said. "That's another thing I know for sure."

❀

"Okay, let's get started," I said to myself. I finally finished my English paper. Now I had a few minutes to start planning Dad's party before Lauren was due over to study for our history test.

I sat on my bed with my laptop beside me and a book called *Easy Breezy Entertaining with Dori*

Weiss open in front of me. I'd bought it at the bookstore that morning. I figured I could use a little help and Dori Weiss was a famous TV hostess.

"Before you plan your party, ask yourself these questions," Dori wrote. "What is the purpose of the party?"

I typed the answer into my computer. "To celebrate Dad's promotion."

"Who is the party for?"

"Dad."

"Who will be invited?"

I typed in a guest list: Mom, Dad, me, Ashley, Aunt Tess, Uncle Jack, and Dad's friends from work—Dave Kramer and wife and Beth Twitchell and husband. Then I made a note: Get Kramer and Twitchell addresses and phone numbers from Mom.

Okay. So far so good. I skipped the rest of the questions and went to the chapter called "Dinner Party Ideas."

"Is your dinner in honor of someone?" Dori asked. "Why not make a meal of his or her favorite foods?"

Hmmm . . . good idea, I thought. I typed a list of all Dad's favorite foods: sardines, guacamole, goose liver pâté, shrimp fra diavolo, beef burritos, Thai curry, black-eyed peas, sausages and onions, Cap'n Crunch cereal, peanut butter ice cream . . .

Blech. Dad has very gross taste in food, I thought. But this party isn't for me, it's for Dad. So if this is what he likes, that's what I'll make.

"What better way to celebrate your guest of honor than with a statue of that person?" Dori suggested. "Make a sculpture out of vegetables and fruits. A lettuce head, blueberry eyes, carrot nose, tomato mouth. Be creative! Set a bowl of dip near your sculpture and you have a statue and appetizer all in one!"

I giggled. A Veggie Dad? *That could be cute,* I thought. I could even make potato-peel curls for hair. I wasn't sure about the idea of people eating him with dip, but Dori was the expert. She must know what she's talking about.

I looked up the recipes and made a grocery list, storing it all on my computer. First ingredients: twelve cloves of garlic and ten chili peppers.

Hot and spicy, just how Dad likes it, I thought. *This is going to be great!*

chapter eight

DO YOU CLICK?
THE LOVE LINK QUESTIONNAIRE
SECTION ONE: WHO I AM
NAME: Malcolm Freeman
AGE: 16
GRADE: 11
SCHOOL: Bayside High
HOBBIES AND INTERESTS: reading,
horticulture, medical oddities, herpetology,
the French horn, the theremin, the history
of cooking and food, the War of 1812,
hairstyles through the ages, flags and
national anthems, unusual brain disorders,
lightbulbs, moths, genetics, dog racing,
leisure-suit design, sports (shotput, javelin,
curling, luge, Mexican wrestling) . . .

I sighed and shook my head. I was sitting in the

Website office after school on Monday, reading Malcolm's questionnaire. The list of interests went on and on. I had to stop reading after "collecting X-ray specs." Okay, Malcolm, I get the picture!

FAVORITE THINGS:
BOOK: Tie: Weird New Jersey and Beyond, Guinevere and Lancelot: European Names from the Middle Ages
MOVIE: Plan 9 from Outer Space
BAND: Monty Zweeben's French Horn Orchestra featuring Mona Duval on the Theremin
SONG: "Froggy Went A'Courtin'"
COLOR: Carmine
FOOD: Pizza
SCHOOL SUBJECT: English
TEACHER: Mr. Danvers
ARTIST: Hans Holbein the Younger
ACTOR: Bugs Bunny
ACTRESS: Ann-Margret
TV SHOW: Reruns of The Mickey Mouse Club
ANIMAL: Three-toed sloth
HISTORICAL PERIOD: 1766–1776 (the ten years leading up to the American Revolution)
WAY TO WASTE TIME: Watching my friend Ashley try to match up losers

I took a deep breath. *This isn't going to be easy, Ashley,* I told myself. *But you can do it. Somehow, somewhere there's a girl for Malcolm. At least he likes pizza. But "Froggy Went A'Courtin'"? Is he serious? He'll never get the clincher, that's for sure.*

I graphed Malcolm's answers and tested them against a few girls on the Website. Nothing. He had nothing in common with any of them. And I'd decided that I wouldn't match people with nothing in common anymore.

Then I thought of my old notebooks at Click. Maybe there'd be somebody in there for Malcolm. Somebody who hadn't signed on to the Love Link yet.

I headed over to Click. Malcolm was working behind the counter. I took a table in the corner, far away from him, so he couldn't see what I was doing.

This job was beyond the Love Link. It required the personal touch. I was going to have to hand-match Malcolm.

I combed through the notebooks, thinking about Malcolm's quirks. What kind of girl would he like? What kind of girl would like him?

She'd have to be smart, I thought, *and interested in a lot of things, like he is.* They don't have to be the same things, necessarily—how could they be? What kind of girl is interested in dog racing? Come to think of it, what kind of teenage boy is interested in dog racing?

I flipped past cheerleaders whom Malcolm would make mincemeat out of and bookworms who seemed too dull for him. Then I saw her. The one. *This is it*, I thought. *It's as close as I'm going to get.*

Her name was Alexis Byrne. *She's cute,* I thought as I studied her photo. Her straight dark hair was a little limp, and she could use a new pair of glasses—the ones she was wearing were kind of heavy for her face. But with a little help, she could be very pretty.

I glanced across the room at Malcolm. He was no Greek statue himself. I didn't think he'd be too picky about looks. It was brains he was more interested in.

Her interests included reading—a match! not that reading was so uncommon—writing poetry, collecting vintage postcards from the 1940s and '50s, and science. Her favorite subject was biology, but her favorite book was Shakespeare's collected plays.

Hmm . . . this could work, I thought. *She has lots of different interests, just like Malcolm. She's obviously smart.*

I read further on her questionnaire. Under "Why you should get to know me" she wrote, "The real question is, why should I get to know you?"

"My goal for this year is: just to make it through the tenth grade without losing my mind."

"I'm looking for someone who: can take it as well as he can dish it out."

This is perfect, I thought as I carried her questionnaire to the nearest computer. She's sarcastic! It's got to work!

I fed her answers to the Love Link, graphed them, and pressed the button to see what the theory would say. Would they get a heart or a skull and crossbones?

The graph turned red and morphed into a heart. Yes! We had a match!

I had to stop myself from jumping up and down with excitement. I didn't want to scare off Malcolm. The hard part was still to come. I had to get Malcolm to go along with this.

Careful, Ashley, I said to myself. *This is a delicate operation. It must be done with the utmost tact.*

I approached Malcolm at the coffee counter.

"What's new?" I said.

He glared at me. "What are you up to, Ashley? Did you really come over here just to ask me what's new?"

I smiled sheepishly. No use trying to fool Malcolm.

"Look," I said. "I found a girl I think you'll like. According to the theory, it's a very promising match!"

"No." He scowled. "Forget it."

I held up Alexis's picture. He stared at it for a second. I thought I saw a flicker of interest dart across his face. But he said, "Ashley, I told you I won't go on any dates."

He's interested, I thought. *I can tell. He's just shy. He needs a little push. He'll thank me for it later.*

"I know you're not interested, Malcolm," I said. "But do it for me. Please? I need to prove the greatness of my theory, and you can help me do it!"

"I'd feel ridiculous," he said. I caught his eyes straying back toward Alexis's picture. "I filled out the questionnaire for you. Isn't that enough?"

"Take a chance, Malcolm," I pleaded. "What have you got to lose? Listen, if you're so sure you're right and I'm wrong, prove it. All you have to do is go out with Alexis once. If you don't like her, you never have to see her again and you can tell me you told me so. I'll admit that my theory didn't work for you."

I dangled the picture in front of him. He stared at it helplessly.

I've got him, I thought. *He's definitely interested in her. I've just got to get him to admit it.*

"What if I do like her?" he asked.

"Then that will be great!" I said. "You'll just keep going out with her. So, you see, it's win-win for you."

"But if I don't like her, you'll admit your theory

is a failure," he said. "A complete and utter failure."

"Yes," I agreed.

"All right," Malcolm said. "I can't believe I'm saying this. But I'll do it. I'll go out with this Alexis person once."

Yes! I thought. *I only hope Alexis won't say no!*

chapter nine

"Is that her?" Mary-Kate pointed out a girl with lank dark hair and heavy black-rimmed glasses sitting across the courtyard from us. She wore a dowdy calf-length skirt and white blouse. I glanced at the photo of Alexis Byrne in my notebook. It was definitely her.

"She could use a haircut and some new clothes," Mary-Kate whispered. "Under those glasses she's probably really cute."

"That's just what I thought," I whispered back. "Do you think Malcolm will like her?"

Mary-Kate shrugged. "Who knows? Malcolm kind of likes everything. But he also kind of hates everything."

I closed the notebook and put it away in my bag. "Well, here goes. Wish me luck."

"You don't need luck," Mary-Kate said. "You've got the theory!"

"Very funny."

"I wasn't joking," she said. "I was serious. I believe in you, Ashley."

"Thanks," I said. "I guess I'm feeling a little touchy about the theory lately."

I walked across the courtyard. Alexis looked up at me.

"Excuse me," I began, "but are you Alexis Byrne?"

She nodded. "Yes. And you're Ashley Olsen. I recognize you from your picture on the Love Link."

I grinned. "That's me, all right. I found your questionnaire at Click and decided to take on your case personally."

"Really? How very nice of you," Alexis said. I thought I heard a little snobbery in her voice. I didn't expect that from someone so dowdy. Plus, most of the kids at school were pretty friendly.

"Uh, yes," I said, feeling a little nervous now. "I think I've found the perfect guy for you."

She perked up a little. "Who is it?" she asked.

"Malcolm Freeman," I told her. "Do you know him?"

"Not really," Alexis said. "The name sounds kind of familiar. What does he look like?"

I hesitated. I thought Malcolm was kind of cute in his own way, but he wasn't most people's idea of a dreamboat. "Um, well, he's slim—" *like a scarecrow*, I thought. "And he has brown hair that kind of hangs in his face sometimes like a rock star's—" *or a shy guy who doesn't want you to look at him.* "He's kind of pale. You might have seen him at Click. He works there."

Alexis nodded. "Oh, that guy who makes coffee behind the bar? That's who you want to fix me up with?"

"Yes!" I said brightly, hoping my enthusiasm would rub off on her. "He's a great guy. He's really smart and nice—" She was looking a little doubtful, so I decided to make it easier for her. "If you're nervous about it, you and Malcolm could double date with me and my boyfriend this weekend. What do you think?"

"You and your boyfriend?" Alexis said. "Who's that?"

"Aaron Moore," I said.

"You're going out with Aaron Moore?" Alexis asked. I had a feeling she'd know who he was. Every girl in school knew who Aaron was.

"We just started dating," I told her. "I think you'll really like Malcolm," I added. "I applied my Theory of Compatibility to the two of you, and you got a great score!"

Alexis didn't say anything for a few minutes. I held my breath.

"Well, why not?" Alexis finally said. "All right. I'll go out with Malcolm."

"Great!" I cried. "Why don't you meet me at Click after school today and I'll introduce you to him?"

"Sounds good," Alexis agreed. "See you then."

I turned around and flashed Mary-Kate an A-OK sign as I speed-walked back to her.

"She said yes," I whispered to Mary-Kate when I reached her. "I'm halfway there."

"Yeah," Mary-Kate said. "Your theory is practically proven! All you have to do is get Malcolm and Alexis to fall in love. How hard could it be?" She grinned mischievously at me.

"I know, I know," I admitted. "But just imagine— what if it *did* work out! I'd be so happy for Malcolm!"

"So would I," Mary-Kate agreed.

"Oh, Ashley, this is so exciting!" Lauren said.

"Shhh!" I scolded her. "Not so loud! You don't want to make Malcolm nervous."

"Sorry," Lauren whispered.

"It *is* exciting, though," Mary-Kate said.

"I wouldn't miss it for anything," Brittany agreed.

Mary-Kate, Brittany, and Lauren had gathered at Click that afternoon to witness the meeting of Malcolm and Alexis. I was afraid their presence would scare off Malcolm—they were being pretty obvious about why they were there. But I couldn't keep them away. Click was a public place, after all. And it was nice to have company. I was nervous, too.

"See how he keeps looking up every time the door opens?" Brittany said. "He doesn't usually do that."

"And he keeps rubbing the counter with his rag, the same spot, over and over," Mary-Kate noted. "He's definitely nervous."

"Leave poor Malcolm alone," I cried. "Stop watching him every second! It doesn't help!"

"You're worse than we are," Brittany said. "You crane your neck to see who comes in every time the door opens."

"Well, I have to greet Alexis when she gets here, don't I?" I huffed.

The bell on the front door jingled, and in walked Alexis. She had pinned her hair back with a barrette and put on a little lip gloss.

"She fixed herself up to meet Malcolm," Lauren whispered. "That's a good sign!"

I jumped up and hurried to greet her. "Hi, Alexis," I said. "You look nice."

"Thank you," she said crisply. She seemed to think I didn't mean the compliment sincerely, but I did.

I led her to the coffee counter. Malcolm was still rubbing that spot, pretending he didn't notice us.

"Malcolm," I said. "I'd like you to meet Alexis Byrne."

He looked up at last through a curtain of hair. "Hey. Nice to meet you."

"Nice to meet you, too, Malcolm," Alexis said. She settled on a stool. "I read your Love Link questionnaire. It was definitely the most interesting one on the site."

"Heh." Malcolm shyly half laughed. "Thanks."

"Well, I'll leave you two alone to talk," I said. I went back to my table, which Mary-Kate had purposely chosen for its good view of the counter and easy eavesdrop-ability.

"So far so good," I whispered, picking up a magazine. "I think I'll read for a while. How about you guys?"

Brittany pulled a book out of her bag. "I'm definitely up for some reading," she agreed. "Nice, quiet reading."

Mary-Kate and Lauren giggled as they snatched up a couple of magazines. We hid our faces behind them and strained to hear what Malcolm and Alexis were saying.

"So, um, you sure have a lot of interests," Alexis said to Malcolm. "I never met anyone who was into Mexican wrestling before."

"I guess you've never been to Mexico, then," Malcolm said. "Lots of people there dig it."

"That makes sense," Alexis said.

I peeked over my magazine. Malcolm was still hiding behind his hair. *Show your face!* I silently urged him. *Don't be so shy!*

Luckily, Alexis didn't give up easily. "What's a theremin?" she asked. "Some kind of musical instrument?"

Malcolm nodded. "It was invented by this Russian guy, Leo Theremin. It makes an electronic tone. You control the sound by moving your hands closer or farther away from these two antennas—"

"But what does it sound like?" Alexis asked.

Malcolm started to come out from behind his hair. I think he couldn't believe another person was actually this interested in the theremin.

"It makes an eerie sound, like a UFO," he explained. "They used it a lot in old science fiction movies in the 1950s."

"Cool," Alexis said. She picked up a book that was sitting on the counter and glanced at the cover. *"The Secret Life of Plants,"* she read aloud. "Are you reading this?"

"Uh-huh," Malcolm replied.

"I read this last summer," Alexis said. "Isn't it great? It inspired me so much, I wrote a whole cycle of poems about it. It really made me think about, like, you know, do plants have feelings?"

Malcolm lifted his head, and I thought I caught

a glimmer of interest in his eye. "He's impressed," I whispered to Mary-Kate. "Now we're getting somewhere."

Malcolm leaned his elbows on the counter. "I think plants do have feelings," he said. "Why wouldn't they? They're alive, just like we are."

Alexis leaned across the counter until her face was close to Malcolm's. "You know, you're very unusual," she said. "I can really talk to you. It's almost like we're soul mates."

Whoa, slow down there, Alexis, I thought. She was starting to come on pretty strong. I was worried she'd scare Malcolm and he'd back off.

I glanced at Mary-Kate. She raised her eyebrows. Brittany and Lauren were stifling giggles.

Then Malcolm stunned us all.

"I am unusual," he told Alexis. "Seems like you are, too." He paused. "Want to go out with me tomorrow night?"

I gasped, then quickly clapped a hand over my mouth. This was going better than I thought it would. Malcolm actually asked Alexis out!

chapter ten

"**D**id you hear that, Ashley?" Lauren asked.

"Shhh!" I whispered. "I want to hear her answer!"

The four of us sat perfectly still behind our magazines. What would Alexis say?

"Tomorrow night? Sure. Sounds good." She grabbed a slip of paper and scribbled on it with a pen. "Here's my phone number," she said, pushing the paper across the counter to Malcolm. "Give me a call."

She turned around and looked toward my table. "Bye, girls," she said with a little wave.

"Bye, Alexis," I said. "See you at school tomorrow."

She walked out. Mary-Kate, Brittany, Lauren, and I looked at each other. I was afraid to look at Malcolm. I thought I would burst!

"Hey—it's awfully quiet over there," Malcolm called to us. "Aren't you girls usually yapping away about boys or clothes or something? What's the deal, huh?"

"What?" Brittany snapped. "How dare you stereotype us that way! Just because we're girls you think all we care about is boys or clothes? We were actually discussing philosophical issues. Like whether plants have feelings."

"Brittany!" I kicked her under the table.

She tried to act innocent. "What?"

I made a face at her. Then I got up from the table and went over to Malcolm.

"How did it go?" I asked.

"As if you didn't know," he said.

"Do you like her?" I pressed.

"She's okay," he replied. But he smiled, and I could tell he liked her. He *really* liked her.

❀

"Mary-Kate, do you have a second?" Ashley asked. "I'm so excited, I can hardly concentrate on my homework."

"Come on in," I said, slamming my history textbook shut. "I could use a break."

Ashley walked into my room and sat on my bed.

"This proves it," Ashley continued. "For sure. My theory is definitely genius. I mean, Malcolm! The first girl I fix him up with and he really likes her! I think she likes him, too, don't you?"

I hesitated. Something about Alexis gave me a

funny feeling, but I wasn't sure what it was. And I didn't want to dampen Ashley's excitement. I knew how much this meant to her. Still, I had to be honest.

"She seems to like him," I said. "But don't jump to conclusions, Ashley. They haven't even gone on one date yet."

"But it's going to work out great, I can tell!" Ashley bounced up and down on my mattress.

"I hope so," I said.

She stopped bouncing and stared at me. "What? You're thinking something. What is it?"

I sighed. "It's nothing. I'm just not sure about Alexis, that's all. She strikes me as a little strange."

"So?" Ashley said. "Malcolm's a little strange, too. That's why they're so perfect for each other! I matched them myself, using my fabulous theory, which never fails!"

I shot her a look.

"Okay," she conceded. "My theory never fails when it's done right. And this time I did it perfectly."

"All I'm saying is, let's wait and see."

"You want to bet?" Ashley offered. "I'll bet you Malcolm and Alexis will turn out to be a happy couple. If I'm right, I get the Mustang to myself for a whole week. But if it doesn't work out between them, you get it for a week."

"It's a deal," I agreed. "Although I hate to bet

against Malcolm. I really do want him to be happy."

Her eyes fell on the book on my night table, *Easy Breezy Entertaining*. "How are Dad's party plans coming?" she asked.

Party plans? "Uh, oh, great, great," I said even though I hadn't done anything. I'd looked through the Dori Weiss book and entered some ideas into my computer. But I hadn't actually *done* anything yet.

"You've sent out the invitations, right?" Ashley asked. "The party's only a week away."

"Right, right," I said. "Don't worry, it's all under control." *Mental note to self—send out invitations immediately! Like, as soon as Ashley leaves the room!*

"And make sure you order the flowers and the cake ahead of time," she reminded me. "They like about a week's notice."

"I'm all over it," I said, vowing to find a bakery and a florist and call them first thing in the morning.

I've really got to get started on this, I realized. *This party isn't going to plan itself!*

❀

"Hey, Ashley," Malcolm said at lunch the next day. "What have you got for me today?"

I pulled a sandwich out of my bag and passed it across the cafeteria table to him. "Freshly roasted turkey with cranberry sauce on raisin bread," I told him. "Okay? We had turkey for dinner last night."

"Excellent," he said, unwrapping the sandwich.

"So, you're going out with Alexis tonight, huh?" I said. I saw no point in trying to be subtle.

He nodded. "We're going to a lecture at the university. 'How Electricity Changed Civilization.'"

"Sounds interesting," I said. "So, um, what are you going to wear?"

He shot me a wary look. "I don't know, clothes?"

"Don't get touchy," I said. "I just want to make sure you're comfortable on your date."

"Comfortable? If I wanted to be comfortable, I wouldn't go on the date at all."

"You know what I mean," I said.

He set down the sandwich. "No, Ashley, I don't. What do you mean?"

"Well, um . . ." Did I have to come right out and say it? I wasn't sure Malcolm knew what to do on a date. I had a feeling he hadn't had much dating experience.

"You think I've never been on a date before, don't you?" Malcolm said. "Well, I have, so I don't need any advice from you, Coach."

"Who did you go out with?" I asked. As far as I knew, he'd never been out with anyone from Bayside High.

"A girl."

"Come on. Who was she?"

"You don't know her."

"Well, where did you take her?"

"To a dance."

"At Bayside?"

"No. At her school. She goes to St. Mary's."

"Come on, Malcolm," I pleaded. "Tell me who it was."

"Her name is Maggie," he said.

"Maggie what?" I prodded.

"Maggie Freeman."

My eyebrows shot up. "Maggie Freeman? She has the same last name as you!"

Malcolm crumpled his sandwich wrapper into a ball and threw it on the table. "Oh, all right, I'll admit it. She's my cousin, okay? She didn't have a date for her school dance and my mother made me go with her. And that's the only date I've ever been on. Satisfied?"

"Sorry, Malcolm," I said. "I didn't mean to pry."

"Ha!" He laughed. "Look, don't worry, Ashley. I'm not a total geek. I can be Mr. Cool when I have to. Cool and smooth."

He stood up, flipped up the collar of his button-down shirt, turned on his heel, and slouched away. Then he tripped over a chair and sent it clattering to the floor.

People looked up and stared at him.

Malcolm got up, then reached down to pick up the chair. He turned back to me, flashed me a thumbs-up sign, and repeated, "Cool and smooth."

Real smooth, I thought as he pushed his glasses up his long nose and left the room.

I'm not worried. Not worried at all.

chapter eleven

"Ashley? Who are you looking for?" Aaron asked. It was Thursday morning and I was scanning the halls for a certain someone who'd just had his first real date the night before.

"Malcolm," I told Aaron. "I can't wait to hear how his date with Alexis went last night."

"Yeah, that should be good," Aaron joked.

"Aaron!" I said. "Are you making fun of my friend Malcolm?"

"No way," Aaron said. "I like the guy. I can't wait to hear about his date, either. I'm just saying there's probably going to be a good story in there somewhere. Tell me all about it at lunch today?"

"Yes," I promised. "Unless Malcolm is there. Then he can tell you about it himself."

The bell rang. "See you later," Aaron said as he hurried off.

I finally spotted Malcolm between second and

third period, when we both had fifteen minutes free.

"So?" I asked as we sat in the cafeteria with cans of soda. "How was it?"

"Pretty good," Malcolm said, hiding behind his hair. But I thought I saw his face redden. *He likes her!* I thought.

"What happened?" I prodded.

"We went to the lecture, and she actually liked it. I mean, she wasn't bored or just pretending to like it the way most girls would. And then we went out for burgers. Ashley, I can talk to her about anything—even the history of the lightbulb! And she doesn't think it's weird or boring."

He was glowing. I puffed up a little, proud of myself and my theory. It was working! Malcolm actually liked Alexis!

"When are you going to see her again?" I asked.

Malcolm shrugged. "I'm not sure. Maybe not until our double date on Saturday. She said she might stop by Click to see me this afternoon."

"Excellent!" I said. "Maybe Mary-Kate and I will come by, too."

"Oh, great," he said. "You're going to spy on me again?"

"No," I insisted, although I guess that was one way to put it. "Click is our regular hangout, remember? We go there all the time. They have good coffee. We don't go there just to eavesdrop on you and your new girlfriend."

"She's not my girlfriend," Malcolm said.

"Yet," I put in.

"Whatever," he said. "See you."

As I watched Malcolm walk away, I thought his slouch looked a little straighter than usual.

Yes! I thought. *The miracle theory has done it again!*

"It's almost five o'clock," Mary-Kate said, glancing at her watch. "I've got to go home soon. I still have to look up all the recipes for Dad's dinner."

"Are you sure you don't need any help?" I asked her.

She shook her head. "No, no, I've got it under control."

We were hanging out at Click, having coffee after school. I wanted to see if Alexis would stop by to visit Malcolm. So far she hadn't shown up.

"Why hasn't Alexis come in yet?" Mary-Kate asked. "Malcolm is looking a little discouraged."

I studied Malcolm's posture. It did seem to get slouchier as the afternoon wore on. But that was probably normal.

"He always looks like that," I assured Mary-Kate. "Anyway, Alexis didn't promise him she'd come. Maybe something important came up. Or

79

maybe she doesn't want to seem too available."

"I guess," Mary-Kate said.

"I'll go talk to him," I said. I approached the counter. "Hey, Malcolm," I said.

"Hey," he muttered.

"Why don't you give Alexis a call?" I suggested. "See if she'll go out with you tonight."

"Why would she want to go out with me tonight if she didn't want to see me this afternoon?" he asked.

"I'm sure she wanted to see you," I said. "Maybe she couldn't for some reason. Or maybe she's playing hard to get."

"I don't know," he said. "I don't want to push too hard—"

"It's not being pushy," I insisted. "It's just showing you're interested. Girls love that." I pulled my cell phone out of my pocket and handed it to him. "Call her."

He sighed. "Okay. But you can't stand there and listen. Go back to your table."

"I'm going, I'm going," I said. I scurried back to Mary-Kate. "He's calling her."

We watched nervously as he talked on the cell phone. *That's right,* I silently coached him. *Be charming and funny. Not too desperate . . .*

He clicked off and walked over to our table. "Here you go," he said, handing the phone back to me.

"Well?" Mary-Kate and I both asked in unison.

"None of your business," Malcolm said, but his mouth curled upward slightly.

"Malcolm!" I protested.

"Okay, okay. She's meeting me later tonight. We're taking my telescope out to the beach to look at constellations."

"Ooh! Very romantic," I said.

"Don't get used to this, Ashley," he warned. "I'm not giving you the play-by-play of every date I go on forever. After Saturday night, I'm cutting you off."

I grabbed my throat, pretending to be dying of thirst. "No! You can't do that! How will I survive?" I teased.

"Not my problem," Malcolm said, and he went back to work—smiling.

chapter twelve

"**S**orry, Ashley." Malcolm folded his arms as he sat across the table from me in the cafeteria the next day. "No date details until I get my daily lunch treat."

"Okay, okay," I agreed, fishing through my lunch bag. "Here." I offered him a tangerine.

"Is that the best you can do?" he asked.

I rolled my eyes and rummaged around some more until I found a small package of chocolate chip cookies. "How's this?" I asked, handing over the cookies.

"Better," he said, taking them. "You've really slacked off on the treats, Ashley. It's supposed to be payment for setting up your fabulous Web page, remember? One week of lunch treats in exchange for hours of expensive cyber-consulting? But I'll let you off easy since today is the last day."

"Gee, thanks," I said. "Now spill. And I want details."

He looked embarrassed. "It was fun," he confided. "I set up my telescope on the beach. There was no moon, so you could see the stars pretty well. I showed her the constellations. She knew all the Roman myths that go with them and she told me the story behind each one. I already knew the myths, but I liked the way she told them."

I smiled. Alexis was breaking through his defenses pretty quickly.

"So you like her?" I asked.

"No. I like to spend as much time as possible with people I hate."

He liked her!

"I think I might ask her to the spring dance," he added. "I always wanted to take someone I hate to a dance."

"That's excellent!" I cheered.

I'd never seen Malcolm like this before. Alexis was transforming him from a very negative person into a somewhat less negative person! I couldn't wait to see them together on our double date Saturday night.

❋

"There's Alexis," Mary-Kate whispered as we left the gym that afternoon.

Alexis walked toward us. Her hair was tied back with a scarf and she was wearing a cute pair of jeans and a cropped top.

"She looks better than usual, don't you think?" I whispered to Mary-Kate, who nodded.

"Malcolm must be good for her," she said.

Alexis waved when she saw us and walked over to meet us. "Hi, girls," she said. "I can't wait for our date tomorrow night, Ashley."

"Me, too," I said. "Aaron thought we could all go see *The Dark Circle*. It's supposed to be really scary."

"I read kind of a bad review of it in the newspaper," Alexis said. "But I'm sure it will be fine. It doesn't matter to me what movie we see. So what are you going to wear?"

"Um, I hadn't thought about it," I admitted. "Nothing fancy. It's just a movie. Maybe we'll go out for pizza afterward or something."

"I just bought a cute new dress," Alexis said. "Do you think a dress would look too fancy?"

I shrugged. "It depends on the dress, I guess. If you feel comfortable in it, I'm sure it will be fine."

"You know how some guys like girls who dress up, and some guys like it better when girls just wear jeans all the time?" Alexis went on. "That's what I'm trying to figure out."

"Actually, I'm not sure how Malcolm feels about stuff like that," I admitted. "I don't think he pays a lot of attention to fashion."

"Well, what about Aaron, then?" Alexis asked.

"What kind of girl does he prefer, dressy or casual?"

I'd never wondered about this before, and I wasn't sure how to answer. "I don't think Aaron thinks about it," I told her. "I'm sure whatever you wear will be fine."

"Well, okay, I guess," she said. "See you tomorrow night!"

She flounced away, heading for the gym. "I don't know about her," Mary-Kate said as we watched her.

"What?" I asked. "She's obviously excited about tomorrow night. I think she really likes Malcolm. She's just a little unsure of herself."

"That's what's weird about her," Mary-Kate said. "Her questions make her sound unsure of herself. But the way she asks them is very confident. I mean, the tone of her voice and everything. It's a strange combination."

"Strange, weird, whatever, I don't care," I said. "She likes Malcolm. Malcolm likes her. My theory matched them and it's working. Even Malcolm is ready to admit that I'm right!"

"I can't wait to hear about the date tomorrow night," Mary-Kate said. "It's going to be a doozy. I can just tell."

❀

Okay, Mary-Kate, I said to myself. *Dad's party is only a few days away. Better get moving.*

I was in pretty good shape, I thought. I'd

planned the menu and entered a long grocery list on my laptop, ready to print out when I needed it. Now, if I could just find my laptop . . .

I rummaged around my desk. Where was it? Oh, yes. I took it to school yesterday. I must have left it in my backpack.

I opened my backpack and pulled out some textbooks. No laptop.

Oh, no, I realized, my heart sinking. *I left my laptop at school!* I put it in my locker after lunch. I meant to bring it home, but I forgot! Now I wouldn't be able to get it until Monday. And I had to do my shopping today, or I'd never get everything ready in time for the dinner *and* have a chance to develop and print the roll of film I'd taken for the contest. I was sure I'd gotten at least one fantastic picture at the beach and I couldn't wait to see the shots.

No need to panic, I told myself. *This is not a disaster. I can remember most of the grocery list. When I get to the supermarket, it will all come rushing back to me.*

Sure it will, a little voice in my head sniped. I squelched the voice. It was not helpful.

I jumped in the Mustang and headed for the supermarket. I grabbed a cart and wheeled it down the aisles. The supermarket suddenly looked huge. Why hadn't I ever noticed how big it was before?

"Let's see, I'm making guacamole, so I need avocados," I said to myself, grabbing a half dozen avocados and tossing them into the cart. "And there were a lot of spices on the list. . . ." I loaded up on onions, garlic, and peppers. I bought vegetables for the Veggie Dad sculpture, and chicken, shrimp, and sausages—whatever I could think of.

I'm sure I can pull something together out of all of this, I thought, surveying the huge mound of groceries in my cart. But just to be safe I grabbed a box of Cap'n Crunch, Dad's favorite cereal. After all, Dori Weiss had suggested serving your guest of honor his favorite food. And as far as Dad was concerned, you could never go wrong with Cap'n Crunch.

I went home and unloaded all my bags of groceries. Time to start cooking. But now I had a new problem—all the recipes were on my computer, too.

That's okay, I told myself, pulling cookbooks off the kitchen shelf. *I'll just look them all up again.*

I frantically flipped through the cookbooks, trying to remember which recipes I'd chosen. I borrowed Ashley's computer to look up the recipes I'd found online.

This is going to take all day, I realized. And I had to run out and get some photo supplies before the art store closed. *Oh, why did I have to leave my stupid computer at school? Maybe I should just start cooking.*

I grabbed the avocados and peeled them. I dumped them into a bowl and tried to mash them up with a fork to make guacamole.

They were rock hard. I stabbed at them until my fork bent.

Oh, no. I didn't take the time to make sure they were ripe before I bought them.

I grabbed a knife and started chopping the avocados up into tiny pieces. I chopped up a few cloves of garlic and added that. I added some onions and spices. I dumped it all into the food processor and pressed the button.

At least it looked like guacamole now. But it didn't taste right. Must need more garlic, I decided. Dad loves garlic. He always said he could never get enough. So if a little was good, a lot must be better.

I hoped.

chapter thirteen

"That movie was much better than I thought it would be," Alexis said as we walked out of the theater. "Did you like it, Aaron?"

"I didn't think it was that scary," Aaron said. "But Ashley did. And I've got the scars to prove it." He held up his hand. The palm was covered with little fingernail marks.

"Well, come on," I said, defending myself. "That part where the girl pulls back the covers on her bed and the monster is lying there? With all the blood everywhere? That was pretty gross."

"I definitely screamed at that part," Alexis said. "And I usually pride myself on not screaming at movies."

"You *definitely* screamed," Malcolm said to her. "My ears are still ringing."

He grinned at her, but she didn't look his way.

"Let's get some pizza," Aaron suggested. "I'm

absolutely *starving*. Pizza okay with you guys?"

"How about Lucio's?" I said. "It's only a few blocks from here."

"Sounds good," Alexis agreed.

Aaron took my hand as we walked down the street. Malcolm moved closer to Alexis, but he didn't take her hand, and she didn't offer it.

I was starting to wonder if this double date was a mistake. Alexis was acting weird. At the movie she insisted on sitting next to Aaron, even though I was closer to the aisle and there were two empty seats next to me. She walked past me and sat on Aaron's other side. Malcolm had to brush past all three of us to sit next to Alexis.

"My brother used to work at Lucio's," Malcolm said. "Don't drink the fruit punch."

"You mean that red stuff that swirls around in a plastic tank?" I asked. "Why not?"

"They used to spit in it," Malcolm reported. "But don't tell anyone."

"Eeww," I said. "That's grosser than the monster in the movie."

"I would never drink that stuff anyway," Alexis said.

"Got any other secrets you want to share with us, Malcolm?" Aaron asked. "Maybe we should go someplace else."

"Naw, everything else is good there, I promise."

We arrived at Lucio's and took a booth. I slid in next to Aaron and we ordered a large pepperoni pie and a pitcher of Coke.

"How's the soccer team doing this year?" Alexis asked Aaron.

"All right," Aaron replied. "We're four and two so far. You guys should come to one of our games."

"I like soccer," Malcolm said. "It's not as exciting as Mexican wrestling, but it's better than football."

"Since when do you know anything about soccer, Malcolm?" Alexis said.

"I know a little," Malcolm replied. "What about you? Since when do *you* know anything about soccer?"

"I read up on it a little," Alexis said, giving Aaron a look from under her lashes.

"Malcolm knows about all kinds of things," I said, trying to support him in front of Alexis. "He's one of the smartest guys I've ever met."

"That's true," Aaron agreed. "Malcolm knows about stuff I didn't even know existed. Like those tiny parasites that live on your skin? Malcolm was telling me all about that at Click one day—"

"But he's not athletic like you are, Aaron," Alexis said. "There are lots of ways of being smart. There's mind intelligence, and then there's, like, body intelligence. . . ."

Malcolm looked down and started playing with

his fork. Aaron flashed me a look that seemed to say, "What is she talking about?"

"Oh, good, our pizza's here!" I said a little too brightly. The waiter set our food down. I put slices of pizza on plates and passed them around. Anything to get Alexis to stop making everybody so uncomfortable.

"Alexis was telling me she makes her own pizza at home," Malcolm said. "She uses a real Italian recipe—right, Alexis?"

"Right," Alexis said. "Maybe you two would like to come over and try it sometime?" She was talking to both of us, but she looked right at Aaron. She bit into her pizza and drew a long string of cheese off the slice. She twirled the cheese around her finger and bit it off. She smiled at Aaron and practically batted her eyelashes.

Aaron pinched my arm and shot me another "What-does-she-think-she's-doing?" look.

I was wondering that myself.

"You know, I think I might want to try out for the girls' soccer team next year," Alexis said. "Do you think you could coach me, Aaron?"

"Um—" Aaron paused, and a look of alarm crossed his face. "I've got to go to the bathroom," he said suddenly. "Ashley, will you let me out?"

I slid out of the booth so he could get out. "Come with me," he said, grabbing my arm.

"Come with you to the bathroom?" I asked like an idiot.

"I'm sure you have to go, too," Aaron said, dragging me away.

We stopped by the pay phones. "Aaron, what is it?" I asked.

"Were you rubbing my foot with your foot just then?" he asked. "Because somebody was rubbing my foot under the table. And I'm just hoping it was you."

"Oh, no." I groaned. "It wasn't me. And I don't think it was Malcolm."

"Alexis is coming on to me!" Aaron whispered. It was kind of funny to see the panic on his face. I thought he'd be used to this. Girls flirted with him all the time. But tonight it was making him very uncomfortable. "You've got to make her stop!"

"Do you think I like it?" I asked. "She's flirting with my boyfriend right in front of me! And not only that, she's ignoring Malcolm. He's not having a very good time."

"Neither am I," Aaron said. "I like Malcolm. And I like you. And this weird girl is making us all very tense."

"I don't understand it," I said. "She really likes Malcolm—I know she does! I don't get why she's acting this way. Maybe she's trying to make Malcolm jealous."

"Maybe she's crazy," Aaron said. "I don't care. Just make her stop!"

I didn't know what to do. How could I make her stop?

I could see our booth from across the room. Alexis and Malcolm were sitting very close to each other.

"Look," I whispered to Aaron. "It looks like they're kissing! Maybe everything will be okay now."

We returned to our table. Malcolm's head was tilted back, and Alexis cradled it in her hands. At first it seemed like they were kissing. But then I realized Malcolm was holding a napkin up to his nose.

"Malcolm has a nosebleed," Alexis announced. "I guess we'd better get him home."

"Malcolm, are you all right?" I asked.

He nodded. "I'll be fine. I just have to keep my head tilted back for a few minutes. . . ."

"I'll take you home, Malcolm," Alexis offered. "Come on, let's go."

Malcolm lifted his head. "I'm sorry, Ashley. See you guys at school Monday."

"Don't worry about it, Malcolm," I said. "Are you sure you'll be okay?"

"I'll take care of him," Alexis promised. She led him out of Lucio's. Aaron sat down in the booth. I collapsed beside him.

"She didn't seem to mind taking care of him," I said. "She must like him. Right?"

Aaron didn't answer. "Might as well finish this pizza," he said. "Now that we can eat in peace."

I didn't feel hungry anymore. I didn't get Alexis. She was a strange girl. *What was she trying to do tonight?* I wondered. *Was she just acting weird? Or was she really flirting with Aaron?*

After Aaron dropped me off that night, I found Mary-Kate in the kitchen. It was a mess.

"What's going on?" I asked.

"I'm just whipping up a few things for Dad's dinner," Mary-Kate said. Her face was smeared with something green. It looked like avocado. "You know, preparing things ahead of time. I figured I'd get everything organized this weekend so I'd have time to study for history and get my contest photo done during the week."

Organized? It looked more like the end of the world as we know it. Dirty bowls and pots and pans were piled everywhere, and streaks of that green stuff—*was* it avocado?—covered the counter.

"Where's Mom?" I asked. Dad was still away on his business trip.

"She went to bed," Mary-Kate said. "I'm going to bed in a minute. I've just got to clean up this mess. . . ."

Her voice trailed off as she glanced around the kitchen, frowning.

"I'll help you," I offered. "Otherwise you'll be here all night."

"Thanks," she said. "You can tell me all about your date while we clean. How was it? Is Malcolm totally in love?"

I sighed and picked up a sponge. "It's a long story," I began. "And it has a bloody ending."

"Bloody?" Mary-Kate gasped. "What happened?"

"Malcolm got a nosebleed and had to go home," I told her. "Nothing serious." I picked up a pot. The bottom was covered with some kind of blackened goo-like substance.

"What did you do to this pot?" I asked.

"I was trying to caramelize onions," Mary-Kate explained. "I kind of overcaramelized them." She took the pot out of my hand and ran it under the faucet. "I'll take care of it. You tell me about the date. Start at the beginning."

So I did. And the more I talked about it, the weirder it seemed.

"Malcolm, where have you been?" I asked.

It was Monday afternoon. School was almost over, and I hadn't seen Malcolm all day. I finally found him in the courtyard, lying on the grass, a book open beside him. "Don't you have gym now?"

"Hi, Ashley. I'm cutting gym," Malcolm said. "I'm not feeling up to it. Not that I ever do."

I studied him, worried. His face was even paler than usual. He looked unhappy.

"How long have you been lying here?" I asked.

"Since lunch," Malcolm said.

"But that was two hours ago!" I cried.

"I know," he said. "I'm stuck here. I can't get up off the grass. I don't know why."

"Are you okay?" I asked. "Is it your nose?"

"No, that was nothing," he said.

"What are you reading?" I asked, glancing at the title of his book. "*Love Poems for the Heartbroken?* Oh, no." I didn't like the way this was going. "What's wrong?" I asked.

He covered his face with the open book. "Alexis dumped me."

"What?" I cried. "She dumped you? No—I don't believe it!"

"Believe it," Malcolm said. "It's true."

chapter fourteen

"How could Alexis dump you?" I asked. "What did she say?"

"She said I wasn't her type," Malcolm said.

"That's crazy!" I cried. "You're perfect for her! You're smart and nice and funny . . ."

"She said I wasn't cool enough," Malcolm said.

I was stunned. Not cool enough! Who was Alexis to say that? She wasn't exactly Miss Popularity.

"What's wrong with her?" I asked. "You're totally cool! Can't she see that?"

"I guess not," Malcolm said. "Maybe she's not a big fan of nosebleeders."

"Oh, Malcolm." I felt so sad for him. I couldn't help thinking about Saturday night, and the way Alexis had behaved around Aaron.

She dumped Malcolm because she wants a guy like Aaron! I realized, my anger rising. Is that what she means by cool? How dare she! And how dare she hurt Malcolm this way! I felt like shaking her!

"Malcolm, I'm so sorry," I said. "This is all my fault!"

"Yes, it is your fault." Malcolm sighed. "But I can't really blame you. You were only trying to help me. You didn't know that fixing me up with a girl is impossible. I'm unlovable!"

"Don't say that!" I cried. "You're totally lovable! Alexis is the one with the problem."

"Oh, sure, she's got big problems," Malcolm snapped. "She's cute and smart, and she has that little bump on her nose that's so adorable. . . ."

Uh-oh. This was worse than I thought. "Malcolm, that bump on her nose isn't adorable. It's just a bump. I'm sorry I matched you up with her. She doesn't deserve you!"

Malcolm closed the poetry book and struggled to sit up. "You're right. No girl deserves a skinny, smart-mouth guy who gets nosebleeds on dates."

"Malcolm—"

"If you'll help me to my feet, Ashley, I think I'll stumble home now."

"But what about your shift at Click?" I asked. "Aren't you supposed to work there this afternoon?"

"Yes," Malcolm said, holding out his arms. "Help me up. I'm all stiff."

I helped him to his feet.

"Can I do anything else to help you?" I asked. I

hated seeing him this way. He was so sad he was walking all stooped over like an old man.

"Yes," Malcolm said. "Call Click and tell them I won't be in this afternoon."

"But why? What will I say?"

"Say I'm sick," Malcolm said. "Sick of everything."

"Hey, Ashley! Do you want to go to the mall this afternoon?" Lauren asked me when the last bell of the school day rang. "I've got a wicked craving for some curly fries."

I shook my head. "I'm meeting Aaron outside," I told her. "We're going for a bike ride. Enjoy your fries!"

"Don't worry, I will," Lauren said. "Call me later!"

I waved to her and hurried out of the school building. I rounded the corner to the parking lot and headed for the bike rack. I thought I saw Aaron standing there, talking to someone.

It's a girl, I realized as I got closer.

It's Alexis!

She was standing very close to Aaron, talking to him. She had him backed up against the bike rack. He looked like he wanted to run away.

What is she doing? I wondered, quickening my pace. I was already furious with her for dumping Malcolm. What was she up to now?

She turned and saw me coming. Then she hurried away.

"What was that all about?" I asked Aaron when I finally reached him.

"Ashley, you're not going to believe this," Aaron said. "Alexis asked me out!"

chapter fifteen

"What?" I cried. "She asked you out? What did she say?"

"She said, 'Aaron, Ashley's nice and all. But you need a girl like me. Somebody out of the ordinary.'"

"She's out of the ordinary, all right," I fumed. I couldn't believe Alexis. When I met her I thought she was a sweet girl. But she was turning out to be a monster! Not only was she mean to Malcolm, she was trying to steal my boyfriend from me!

"What did you say?" I asked him.

"I didn't have time to say anything," Aaron replied. "She ran off when she saw you coming."

I smiled at him, and then I started laughing.

"What's so funny?" Aaron asked.

"You are," I replied. "You should have seen your face when she had you pinned against this bike rack. You looked ready to jump over it and run."

"She scares me," Aaron admitted.

I hugged him. I had nothing to worry about. Aaron wasn't interested in Alexis, and nothing she could do would make him like her.

"Anyway, nobody quacks like Ashley," Aaron added, hugging me back.

"Quack quack," I said.

"Ashley's quacky, and Alexis is wacky," Aaron joked.

"Okay, enough," I said. "Let's go for a bike ride. I need some air."

We rode our bikes home, taking the long way by the beach. We didn't talk much. I had a lot on my mind.

Alexis could flirt with Aaron all she wanted—I knew she'd never be able to steal him away from me. That didn't worry me. But I felt bad about Malcolm.

This whole thing was my fault, I knew. I pushed Alexis on Malcolm for my own sake more than his. I wanted to feel good about my success as a matchmaker. I wanted to prove that my theory worked. But I didn't know Alexis at all. And now it was a total disaster!

I've got to find a way to help Malcolm, I thought. *I've got to make him feel better somehow.*

But how? How could I fix someone's broken heart?

● ● ●

"She did *what*?" Mary-Kate shouted. "She dumped Malcolm? And then she asked Aaron out?"

As soon as I got home, I told Mary-Kate what happened with Alexis. She was in the kitchen, standing next to a tower of vegetables stacked into blobby shapes.

"Mary-Kate, what is that?" I asked, pointing at the tower.

"Veggie Dad," Mary-Kate replied. "Do you like it?"

I stared at it. At the base was some kind of creamy-looking dip stuff studded with cherry tomatoes, carrots, cauliflower, celery, and snow peas. Two long celery stalks jutted out the sides. On the top was a head of lettuce with a carrot nose, pea eyes, and curly potato-peel hair.

It was hideous.

"What is it for?" I asked.

"It's three things in one!" Mary-Kate exclaimed. "It's a sculpture of Dad, made in his honor. It's also the centerpiece for the table and pre-dinner appetizers. Just pick off a piece, swipe it through the dip, and eat!"

"Wow." I didn't know what else to say.

"And it only took me twenty minutes," she added. "Dori Weiss said it would take at least an hour, but I have to go over to the darkroom at school to work on my contest picture. Anyway, I thought I'd better get it done today, because I have so many things left to do tomorrow."

"Good thinking," I said.

"So how is Malcolm doing?" Mary-Kate asked. "Is he upset?"

"Very upset," I replied. "He still likes her! And he thinks he's unlovable."

"Just because a drip like Alexis dumped him?" Mary-Kate cried. Her eyes flashed her steely, determined look. She was getting ready for action. "This is wrong," she said. "And we've got to make it right. Ashley, Malcolm needs your help. He needs some good, old-fashioned Ashley TLC."

"What about Alexis?" I asked.

"Alexis needs to be taught a lesson," Mary-Kate said. "You take care of Malcolm. I'll take care of Alexis. Do you have her phone number?"

"Upstairs on my desk," I said.

Mary-Kate ripped off her apron and marched up the stairs. "I think I'll call a little meeting with her."

Uh-oh, I thought. *Look out, Alexis.*

❀

"Alexis, we need to talk," I said.

I found her trying on clothes at Zipper, a popular boutique in the mall. She'd just stepped out of a dressing room, wearing a short skirt and cropped T-shirt. Definitely a new look for Alexis.

"What are you doing here, Mary-Kate?" she demanded. "How did you find me?"

I'd called her house and her mother told me she was shopping at the mall. But Alexis didn't need to know that.

"That doesn't matter," I said. "I've got to talk to you."

"I've got nothing to say to you," Alexis insisted. "I hardly know you."

"Well, *I* know *you*," I said. "And I have a question I'd like you to answer. How could you dump Malcolm like that?"

She rolled her eyes. "Look, get over it. People break up. What's the big deal?"

"If you make a sincere effort to like someone, that's one thing," I said. "But you were just mean! You led him on and made him think you liked him. Why did you have to be so cruel when you broke up with him? And how could you try to steal Aaron away from Ashley?"

"Do you think I'm the only girl who wants to go out with Aaron?" Alexis said. "Every girl in school has a crush on him! I was never interested in Malcolm. He's just not cool enough for me."

"So why did you go out with him in the first place?" I demanded. "Why did you make him think you liked him?"

"To get to Aaron," Alexis explained. "The double

date with Malcolm and Ashley was my chance to make him notice me."

"You could have found another way," I said. "You didn't have to use my sister and Malcolm."

"Yeah, but it was more fun this way," she said. "I wanted to see if I could get Malcolm to fall for me—and he did. But it was too easy. I got tired of him, so I dumped him."

"You're horrible!" I cried. A couple of customers looked over at us in alarm. A saleswoman walked up and asked, "Is everything all right here, girls?"

"Everything's fine," I said.

"Let me know if you need any help," the saleswoman said, walking away.

"You're horrible," I repeated in a whisper. "You can't go around hurting people just for fun!"

"Grow up, Mary-Kate," Alexis said. "Dating's a game. Either you win or you lose—and I won. Malcolm lost. That's the way it goes. Now, if you'll excuse me, I've got some shopping to do."

She disappeared inside the dressing room.

"You haven't won anything!" I called through the dressing room door. "You'll see! You'll lose in the end!"

I heard her laughing through the door.

What a terrible girl!

chapter sixteen

"What happened, Mary-Kate?" Ashley asked when I got home. "Did you let her have it?"

"I tried my best," I reported. "Unfortunately, she doesn't think she did anything wrong."

"Neither does Malcolm," Ashley said. "That's the worst part. He doesn't see what a bad person she is. He thinks *he's* the bad person."

"We need to open his eyes and show him the real Alexis," I said. "Then maybe he won't feel so bad. Maybe he'll be *glad* she broke up with him."

"Good idea," Ashley said. "We can give her a taste of her own medicine at the same time."

"That's just what I was thinking," I replied. "And I think I know how to do it."

"How?"

"Round up the troops," I said. "I've got some writing to do. We're going to put on a little play."

"A play?" Ashley frowned. "I don't get it."

"You'll see," Mary-Kate said.

❀

"There it is, Ashley," Malcolm said, pointing out the giant blue gorilla up ahead. "King Kone."

I pulled the Mustang into the parking lot. It was a warm night. Malcolm and I were riding around with the top down. What could be more natural than stopping for some ice cream?

The headlights flashed across the ice cream stand as I parked the car. And there at the picnic table, frozen in the headlights like a couple of deer, were Aaron and Alexis.

"Malcolm, look who's here," I cried.

"Well, well," Malcolm said. "Aaron and Alexis."

Aaron jumped to his feet and dropped his ice cream cone. "Ashley! Malcolm! What are you doing here?"

"What are *you* doing here, Aaron?" I demanded. "With *her*!"

Aaron looked nervous. "Ashley, it's not what it looks like—"

"Yes, it *is* what it looks like," Alexis cut in. "Aaron and I are here together—on a date!"

"Aaron—you . . . and Alexis?" I gasped.

"Ashley, we might as well tell him the truth," Malcolm said.

"The truth?" Aaron said. "What truth?"

Alexis laughed. "Don't tell me. You're not cheating

on Aaron with *Malcolm* are you? What a laugh!"

"Why not?" I said. "Malcolm is the greatest guy I've ever met. Ever since I first saw him at Click, I knew it was true love."

"This is great," Alexis said. "You two are perfect for each other! And so are Aaron and I!"

"I'll miss Aaron," I said. "But I guess I have to let him go."

"Ashley, no," Aaron cried. "Nothing happened between Alexis and me. You're the one I want!"

"I'm sorry, Aaron," Malcolm said, taking my hand. "Ashley is mine now."

"Good riddance," Alexis said. "Come on, Aaron. Let's get out of here."

Aaron tugged me away from Malcolm. "You're *my* girlfriend, Ashley."

Alexis yanked one of Aaron's arms. "Aaron, let go of her!" she snapped. "You're supposed to be with me! Why did you ask me out for ice cream if you're in love with Ashley?"

Aaron ignored her. "I had a feeling you liked Malcolm all along, Ashley. I can't compete with him. He's too cool!"

Alexis looked confused. "What?"

Aaron turned to her. "Alexis, please," he begged. "Malcolm used to like you. Win him back. Use your charms to get him back so I can have Ashley again!"

"Forget about Ashley," Alexis said, tossing her

hair. "Let her have Malcolm. You can be with me now."

Aaron shook his head. "Sorry, Alexis. I don't want to be with you. I never did. I was just—" He stopped.

"What?" Alexis demanded. "You were just what?"

"Using you. . ." Aaron finished. "To make Ashley jealous."

"Using me?" Alexis said. "That is so mean! How could you do that?"

"I don't know, Alexis," I said. "How could anybody do something so mean? Why don't *you* tell *us*?"

"But I—" she began. She stopped and looked at Aaron. "What's going on here, Aaron?"

Aaron draped his arm around me. "We just wanted you to see what it felt like."

Alexis stared at Aaron. "You mean you never really wanted to go out with me? You were just pretending?"

"I'm sorry, Alexis," Aaron said. "I did ask you if you wanted to get some ice cream. But I never actually said I wanted to date you."

"But—I just assumed—" she stammered.

"It wasn't very nice of me," Aaron admitted. "But then, you weren't very nice, either, were you, Alexis?"

Alexis stared at us for a moment. Her face was

red and blotchy. She opened her mouth a few times, as if she were going to say something. Then she turned on her heel and stomped away.

"Maybe Alexis should try out the theory again, Ashley," Malcolm said. "Talk about cruel and unusual punishment."

"Very funny, Malcolm," I said. "I'm glad to see you've got your sour sense of humor back!"

❀

Okay, Mary-Kate, don't panic, I said to myself. It was Friday afternoon and I'd finally gotten home from school. I'd stayed late at the darkroom making the finishing touches on my contest picture. When I was done even *I* was impressed. It was a beautiful shot of the sunset over the beach.

But now, as I looked around the kitchen, my heart sank. It was five o'clock. The guests were arriving at seven. I was in serious trouble.

Veggie Dad stood drooping on the dining room table, but he didn't look very appetizing. He also didn't look much like Dad.

Why did I waste time on that stupid Veggie Dad? I thought. *I should have been making actual food!*

Okay. Time to get down to work. I had to go pick up the cake and the flowers. Then I had to print out my recipes and start cooking.

At least I remembered to bring my laptop home with me this time, I thought. I opened up the computer and tried to access my party notes. A message flashed on the screen: FILE CANNOT BE LOCATED.

What? Not again!

I searched the hard drive again.

FILE CANNOT BE LOCATED.

"Stupid laptop!" I muttered. All my party plans were in there! All my recipes!

The box of Cap'n Crunch sat on the kitchen counter. Its red cardboard seemed to blare at me like an alarm.

I've got to do something, I thought. *Or I'll be serving Dad cereal for dinner.*

chapter seventeen

"**M**alcolm, I want to apologize," I said. I found Malcolm back at work at Click on Friday afternoon. He seemed better, but I still felt bad about what had happened with Alexis.

"No need to apologize," Malcolm said. "Hey, I'm a man of the world. Seen it all, done it all. A little heartbreak means nothing to me. Rolls right off my back—"

"Still," I interrupted. I couldn't take much more of his man-of-the-world act. "I was wrong. I pushed you into dating Alexis. You were right to be skeptical."

I reached into my bag and pulled out a wrapped package. "I bought this for you. To make up for what happened."

He took the package. "Thanks, Ashley," he said. "You didn't have to do that. But then again, it's the least you could do after what you put me through."

"Just open it."

He unwrapped the package. Inside was a book, *The Mating Behavior of Insects*.

"It says in there that some female insects kill the males when they're finished with them," I told him. "So you got off easy."

"Heh." He snorted. "I can't wait to read it. I've wanted to get this book for a while, but it's out of print. Where did you find it?"

"At that used book shop on Sunset," I told him.

"Grover's?" he said. "I love that place."

"There was a really nice girl working there who helped me find the book," I told him. "Cute, too."

He looked up at me. "Does she have short brown hair with lots of barrettes in it?" he asked. "And she wears overalls all the time?"

I nodded. "Her name is Sophie. She asked me who the book was for, and when I mentioned your name, she said she knows who you are."

He dropped the book on the counter. "Get out. She knows who I am? How? I never got up the nerve to talk to her."

I started to get excited. As soon as I saw Sophie I knew she was Malcolm's type—and I was right! I felt a match coming on. . . .

"She told me you come into the shop a lot and talk to Grover," I explained. "She asked Grover who you were. She's curious about you."

"About me?" Malcolm's eyes lit up. "She's curious

115

about me?" He paused. "You're kidding, right? This is just a joke, right?"

"Look inside the book," I told him.

He opened the book. Inside, on the title page, Sophie had written her name and phone number.

"Oh. My. God." Malcolm slammed the book shut, then opened it again and stared at the title page. "She wrote down her number? For me? She wants me to call her?"

"Of course she does," I said. "Is that so hard to believe?"

"Well. This is interesting," Malcolm said. I could tell he was trying to keep his cool. "Thank you, Ashley. I'm sorry about the whole Alexis mess. I know you were just trying to help me. It wasn't your fault things didn't work out."

"I shouldn't have pushed you into it," I said. "I realize now that you can't depend on numbers alone to match people up. You need the human factor. You know, that gut instinct."

"'Gut' is a good word for it," Malcolm teased. "As in 'nausea.'"

I grinned. I was so glad to see him happy again—well, maybe "happy" was too strong, but at least not completely miserable.

From now on, the theory would be just the first step. My instincts would make the final judgment.

"I think I'll change the Love Link," I told

Malcolm. "Kids can still log on and test their compatibility with other kids."

They obviously loved filling out the questionnaire—it was getting to be very popular. Ms. Barbour told me that the number of hits on the school Website had gone up forty percent since the launch of "Ashley's Love Link." And from the e-mails and calls I'd gotten, people were starting to take it more seriously.

"But I won't set up any matches without meeting everyone face-to-face first," I continued.

"Do you promise?" Malcolm asked.

I held up my hand and made a solemn vow. "Cross my heart."

"Good for you," Malcolm said. "That way you'll get to meet every loser in school personally!"

"Very funny," I said, but I wasn't really mad.

"It's so much fun to tease you, Ashley," Malcolm admitted. "But thanks for caring about me. And for being such a good friend." He put the book away behind the counter. "Don't get used to hearing a lot of sappy talk from me," he added. "Starting now, I'm going back to my old sarcastic self."

"Good," I said. "I missed the old Malcolm."

"Well, he's back. And I've been letting you off too easy. What's all this lovey-dovey stuff between you and Aaron? You know, the quack quack stuff?"

"It's an inside joke," I said.

"Well, knock it off," Malcolm said. "It's totally gross."

"We'll try not to do it around you," I promised.

"You'd better not," Malcolm warned. "Or I'll let you have it."

"Deal. Now, can I please have a skim mocha latte to stay?"

He scowled. "You people and your fancy coffee drinks. Regular coffee isn't good enough for you?"

He turned away to work the coffee machine. I settled down at a table. Everything was back to normal. Even better than normal. And it felt good.

I got home at five that afternoon. "Mary-Kate!" I called, walking into the kitchen. "How's the dinner going?"

Mary-Kate was sitting at the kitchen table, her head resting on the keyboard of her laptop.

"Mary-Kate! What's wrong?" I asked.

"Nothing is ready," she moaned. "The table isn't even set—"

"But why?" I asked. "What happened?"

"My stupid laptop!" she cried. "It ate all my notes! And everything I made to eat tastes like garlic—way, way too much garlic. And now there's no time to cook anything decent. There's nothing to eat but Veggie Dad!"

I stared at Veggie Dad through the dining room

doorway. He looked like some kind of horrible scarecrow. The carrot nose fell off and bounced on the floor.

I glanced at the clock. It was after five. Mom would be home from work at six and the guests were due to arrive at seven. Dad was supposed to come home from his business trip at seven-thirty—and then, "Surprise!" There was no time to fool around.

Mary-Kate continued. "I had so much to do—studying for my history test and my English paper and my Website articles and the photography contest! I didn't set aside enough time to plan the party. And now I have no choice: I've got nothing to serve for dinner but Cap'n Crunch cereal. Even I can't ruin that."

She paused. "Oh, yes, I can. I forgot to buy milk."

"Don't worry, Mary-Kate," I said. "Just call a catering service!"

"A catering service!" Mary-Kate cried. "The dinner starts in less than two hours! It's way too late for that."

"No, it isn't," I insisted. "Not if you hire Ashley's Last-Minute Catering Service. You get on the phone and round up Brittany, Lauren, Aaron, and Malcolm. We'll all do the cooking. I can whip up my super-easy delicious pasta dish, you can make a salad, and Brittany can make her world-famous brownies! Dad'll love it! You organize the troops. This is going to be one fabulous celebration dinner—with waiters and everything!"

Mary-Kate stood up. "Do you think we can pull it off?"

"Sure we can," I said.

"See, this is why I should have left the whole thing to you in the first place," Mary-Kate said. "I never would have thought of waiters!"

"You'd better hurry," I told her. "Go call everybody and tell them to get over here now!"

She broke into a grin and threw her arms around me. "Thanks, Ashley! You're the best."

She hurried up to her room to call our friends. I rolled up my sleeves and got to work.

"More pasta, sir?" Aaron asked Dad. Mary-Kate and I were sitting at the big dining-room table with Mom, Dad, Uncle Jack and Aunt Tess, and some of Dad's work friends.

Everything looked beautiful. Mary-Kate had set the table with Mom's best dishes. Aaron had brought some flowers for the table. He and Malcolm, wearing aprons, served as waiters, while Brittany and Lauren kept the food warm in the kitchen.

"Thank you, Aaron," Dad said, accepting some pasta. "Girls, everything is delicious!"

"You both did a wonderful job," Mom added. "I hardly recognize my own dining room!"

"The room looks so cozy and romantic," Aunt Tess said.

Lauren had brought a beautiful tablecloth and filled the room with candles. Brittany made a banner with the words, "Congratulations, Mr. Senior Vice President!"

Malcolm grabbed a pitcher and refilled everyone's water glasses. "You should have seen this place an hour ago," he murmured.

"Shhh!" I whispered, kicking him as he passed by. An hour earlier we were all running around like crazy, trying to get the dinner ready. The dining room had looked like a construction site. But the guests didn't need to know that.

"I'd like to propose a toast," Mary-Kate said, standing up. "To my dad—the new senior vice president. Congratulations on your big promotion. You're talented and you work very hard. And on top of that, you're a great guy and a fantastic father. Nobody deserves it more!"

"Hear hear!" everyone echoed around the table, clinking glasses.

Dad beamed. "Thank you. I'd like to propose a toast myself. To my wonderful wife, who helps me so much and makes life at home so happy. And to my two beautiful daughters, Ashley and Mary-Kate.

Thank you for giving me this lovely celebration dinner. You are the most thoughtful daughters anyone could have."

He stood up and raised his glass. Everyone clapped and clinked glasses again. Mary-Kate smiled at me.

When dinner was finished, Aaron and Malcolm cleared the table. Mary-Kate stood up and said, "I'll go see if dessert is ready."

"I'll come with you," I said, and followed her into the kitchen.

"Great dinner party, you guys!" Lauren said.

"We've been watching from here," Brittany added. "Everyone's having a good time, especially your dad. I can tell he really appreciates this."

"It is working out perfectly!" Mary-Kate said as she arranged the brownies on a plate. "You saved the day, Ashley! I owe you a *really* big favor."

I gave Mary-Kate a hug. "I know something you can do for me right now."

"What is it, Ashley?" Mary-Kate asked.

"Promise me you'll *never* make another Veggie Dad."

Mary-Kate giggled and held up her hand. "Cross my heart."

Find out
what happens next in

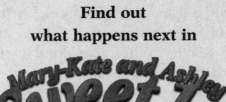

Book 9:
All That Glitters

Mary-Kate stood in the auditorium of the Sunshine Day-care Center. "So, Ashley, is that going to be the set?" she asked, staring at the stage.

On the stage, our friend Brittany was painting scenery for our production of Snow White and the Seven Dwarves. The kids in the play were due to arrive for rehearsal any minute.

"Yes," I said proudly. "Isn't it great, Mary-Kate?"

"Um, I'm Mikki now, remember?" Mary-Kate said.

Brittany and I exchanged a glance. "Right—I forgot," I said. "What do you think of the set, Mikki?"

Mary-Kate wrinkled her nose. "Don't you think it's kind of . . . obvious?"

"Obvious?" I asked. "What do you mean?"

Mary-Kate stepped onto the stage. "Look at this forest. It's all green."

"That's the usual color for trees," Brittany said.

"Yes, but what does this forest stand for?" Mary-Kate asked. "What role does it play in the story? What does it represent?"

Brittany stared at Mary-Kate. "It represents a bunch of trees."

"I think I know what Mary-Kate—I mean *Mikki*—is getting at." I was trying to see her point of view, even though she was starting to bug me. "In the play, the Queen orders the hunter to take Snow White into the forest and kill her. So the forest represents danger."

"Right," Mary-Kate said. "You don't need to paint trees. Everyone knows a forest has trees. Paint the *color*. The *feeling*. Maybe black. Or blood-red."

"*You* paint it blood-red," Brittany snapped. "I just spent two days on this forest, and I'm not doing it over."

Mary-Kate shrugged. "I'm just trying to make the play more interesting, more memorable."

"This is a day-care center," Brittany said, "not Broadway."

Mary-Kate turned to her. "That doesn't mean that we have to be obvious or ordinary, does it?"

Brittany rolled her eyes and went back to painting sets.

"Wait till you meet the kids," I told Mary-Kate, trying to change the subject. "They're so cute! We've already rehearsed a couple of scenes. They have a little trouble remembering their lines, but they're so adorable it doesn't matter."

"I watched the kids working on the set of Diana's movie," Mary-Kate said. "They were cute, too, but they knew their lines cold. They all had acting coaches."

"Well, obviously we can't afford to hire coaches," I said. *That's the tenth time Mary-Kate— Mikki—mentioned Diana,* I thought. *If Mary-Kate says the name 'Diana Donovan' once more, I'm going to scream! Even if Diana is an Oscar-winning actress.*

"I'll help the kids with their lines," Mary-Kate offered. "I learned a lot from watching those coaches." She took another look at the set. "But we have *got* to do something about that background! I learned so much about lighting on the set of Diana's movie—I'm sure I'll come up with something."

I took a deep breath and counted to ten. "Sure . . . Mikki."

There was a clatter in the hallway and then fifteen kids, ages four to six, led by their teacher, Douglas, trooped into the auditorium and up to the stage.

"Hey, kids!" I greeted them.

"Hi, Ashley!" they shouted. They sat down on the stage floor.

"They're all yours, Ashley," Douglas said. "I'm taking a coffee break." He waved to the kids and made his way out of the auditorium. Douglas is twenty-three, stocky, rumpled, and bear-like, with a round face and short dark hair clipped close to his head. The kids love him.

Mary-Kate joined me at the front of the stage. "Kids, I want you to meet someone very special," I announced. "This is my sister, Mikki. She's going to play . . . guess who?"

"The Wicked Queen!" a little boy named Darren called out.

"That's right," I said. Mary-Kate wrinkled up her face, twisted her hands into claws, and screeched out her witchiest laugh. "A-ha-ha-ha-ha! I'll get you, Snow White!" The kids screamed and giggled.

"Ooh! She's scary! She's like a witch!" Darren shouted.

"Mikki knows a lot about putting on plays," I told the kids. "Let's show her the scene we practiced yesterday. Remember? I need my seven dwarves. Stand up, dwarves."

The dwarves stood up. "All right, Mary-K—Mikki," I said, pointing to each child in turn. "Meet the dwarves!"

Mary-Kate grinned. "I can't wait to see your work," she said to them.

Their work? They were kindergartners!

"Okay, kids," I said, leading the dwarves backstage and lining them up. "Remember, this is the beginning of the story. The dwarves are marching home from their work in the mines. They are going home to their cottage in the forest. They are unhappy because the cottage is all messy and none of the dwarves knows how to cook or clean. Okay, begin."

Mary-Kate, Brittany, and I watched as the kids rehearsed their scene. They all looked so serious—and cute!—as they said their lines. I grinned at Brittany. She gave me a thumbs-up.

"All right, all right," I said, clapping my hands to get their attention. "We'll stop there for now. When Lauren gets here we can rehearse some more." I turned to Mary-Kate. "What do you think?"

Mary-Kate frowned. "I think I can help you," she said. "Let me talk to the grouchy dwarf. I'll deal with the shy dwarf later."

Deal with? I thought. "Okay, Mikki," I said, "but remember—they're only little kids." I called to the girl who played the grouchy dwarf. "Come here a minute, please, Hannah. Mikki wants to talk to you."

Hannah marched over and sat on the stage beside Mary-Kate. "Hi, Hannah," Mary-Kate said. "How are you?"

"Fine," Hannah said.

"No, Hannah, you're not fine," Mary-Kate told her. "You're grouchy, remember? Everything stinks! You're always in a bad mood!"

"I'm not grouchy," Hannah protested. "I'm happy!"

"But you are *playing* the grouchy dwarf," Mary-Kate said. "You've got to really get into your part. You have to *be* grouchy, deep down inside. Think for a minute. What is your motivation?"

Hannah looked confused. "I don't know that word," she said.

I nudged Mary-Kate. "Um—Mikki—don't you think you're being a little—"

Mary-Kate ignored me and pressed on. "Close your eyes and think," she told Hannah. "Why is the grouchy dwarf so grouchy? What made her that way? Maybe something happened to her, a long time ago. Something she can never forget—"

Hannah stared up at Mary-Kate. "I forgot to wash my hands before I ate my cookies."

Mary-Kate sighed. "Let's try this. What makes *you* feel grouchy, Hannah?"

Hannah thought for a minute. "When my sister eats all the cookies," she said.

"Good, good," Mary-Kate said. "So when you get up on that stage, keep thinking about that. Think, 'My sister ate all the cookies! That's why I'm so grouchy!' Okay?"

"Okay," Hannah said. Then she toddled back to the other dwarves. "My sister ate all the cookies! That's why I'm grouchy!" she announced.

"Are you sure this is such a good idea?" I asked Mary-Kate. "I mean, Hannah's only five. I think you're confusing her."

"Listen, Ashley, I know what I'm doing. You'll see," Mary-Kate said. "I'll work with each of the kids individually—even the animals. By the time you put on this play, it will have more depth and texture than you ever dreamed!"

"Depth?" I echoed. "Texture? This is a play at a day-care center!"